||||| ||| | ||| ||||| ||| ||||| ||| ||| ||| ||| |||
◁ **P9-BYL-955**

FROM THE
NANCY DREW FILES

THE CASE: Bess answers a romantic personal ad and is mistaken for a mystery woman who is marked for death.

CONTACT: Hank Whittaker, editor in chief of the River Heights *Morning Record.* He agrees to let Nancy work at the newspaper to trace the sender of the strange ad.

SUSPECTS: Lena Verle—*the Personals editor hates Nancy on sight and seems intent on driving her off the case.*

Lucy Price—*the pretty features writer has made an enemy in Lena Verle.*

Steve Beldon—*Bess's blind date turns out to be dangerously bad news.*

COMPLICATIONS: Someone goes after Nancy— and gets Ned instead.

Books in THE NANCY DREW FILES® Series

#1	SECRETS CAN KILL	#17	STAY TUNED FOR DANGER
#2	DEADLY INTENT	#18	CIRCLE OF EVIL
#3	MURDER ON ICE	#19	SISTERS IN CRIME
#4	SMILE AND SAY MURDER	#20	VERY DEADLY YOURS
#5	HIT AND RUN HOLIDAY	#21	RECIPE FOR MURDER
#6	WHITE WATER TERROR	#22	FATAL ATTRACTION
#7	DEADLY DOUBLES	#23	SINISTER PARADISE
#8	TWO POINTS TO MURDER	#24	TILL DEATH DO US PART
#9	FALSE MOVES	#25	RICH AND DANGEROUS
#10	BURIED SECRETS	#26	PLAYING WITH FIRE
#11	HEART OF DANGER	#27	MOST LIKELY TO DIE
#12	FATAL RANSOM	#28	THE BLACK WIDOW
#13	WINGS OF FEAR	#29	PURE POISON
#14	THIS SIDE OF EVIL	#30	DEATH BY DESIGN
#15	TRIAL BY FIRE	#31	TROUBLE IN TAHITI
#16	NEVER SAY DIE		

Available from ARCHWAY paperbacks

THE NANCY DREW FILES

CASE · 20

VERY DEADLY YOURS

Carolyn Keene

AN ARCHWAY PAPERBACK
Published by POCKET BOOKS
New York   London   Toronto   Sydney   Tokyo

AN ARCHWAY PAPERBACK *Original*

An Archway Paperback published by
POCKET BOOKS, a division of Simon & Schuster Inc.
1230 Avenue of the Americas, New York, N.Y. 10020

ISBN: 0-671-68061-7

First Archway Paperback printing February 1988

10 9 8 7 6 5 4 3 2

NANCY DREW, AN ARCHWAY PAPERBACK and colophon
are registered trademarks of Simon & Schuster Inc.

THE NANCY DREW FILES is a trademark
of Simon & Schuster Inc.

Printed in the U.S.A.

IL 7+

VERY DEADLY YOURS

Chapter

One

"Now THIS IS the way to spend the day," Nancy Drew said with a contented sigh as she put down her cup of hot chocolate. She leaned back on the sofa and smiled at her friends.

It was a damp, cold Sunday afternoon. Rain splattered the windowpanes, and wind howled around the corners of the house, but inside Nancy's living room it was warm and cozy. A fire crackled merrily in the grate, and a bowl of red tulips on the mantel made a cheery contrast to the grayness outside.

Nancy and her best friends, Bess Marvin and George Fayne, were just finishing a late brunch and reading the Sunday River Heights *Morning*

1

Record. George was curled up at the other end of the sofa reading about a tennis tournament. In the easy chair closest to the fire, Bess was absentmindedly munching grapes and twisting a lock of her long blond hair as she pored over the Personals column.

"Any news out in the real world, Nan?" asked George, not really expecting an answer.

"Not much, at least not in River Heights. There's a front-page article about a bird's nest in the lobby of City Hall. It's been a slow weekend, I guess—kind of nice for a change."

"You can have the Personals when I'm done," Bess said. "There are all kinds of great things in here. I don't know why you read anything else. To me, the paper *is* the Personals column."

Nancy shook her head. "I never let myself read the good sections until I finish the news. It would be like having dessert before the rest of the meal."

"Speaking of dessert," Bess said, "is there any of that coffeecake left?"

George peered over the top of the sports section. "You seem to be putting those grapes away pretty fast," she said.

Bess snorted. "Health food! If I have to start a diet tomorrow, I might as well have a good time today."

Nancy grinned as she pushed the last piece of coffeecake in Bess's direction. "Well, since you start a new diet *every* day, you might as well eat this and get temptation out of your way."

"Oh, don't make fun of me," Bess said. "If I had a figure like yours, I'd be nicer to all the poor girls who have to think about their weight."

There was nothing wrong with Bess's figure, but Nancy didn't bother arguing with her. She knew it was hopeless. In all the time she had known Bess and Bess's cousin, George, Bess never stopped complaining about her weight. But she had never managed to stick to a diet for more than a couple of hours.

"I see Emerson won its basketball game yesterday, Nan," George said. "Ned must feel great —it says here he scored forty-three points."

"He does feel great," Nancy said. "He called last night to tell me about it." Her boyfriend, Ned Nickerson, was one of Emerson College's star athletes. "And he'll be here tomorrow to tell me about it in person. His last final is over, and he's got three whole weeks of intersession before next term starts. I can't wait!"

"And I bet *he's* glad you're not involved in a case at the moment," Bess chimed in. "How many vacations of his have you actually been able to spend with him?"

Nancy sighed. "Not many." It always bothered her that her work as a private detective took her away from Ned so often. She knew that he understood—most of the time—but it was still hard when her job came between them. She decided to change the subject. "So what's going on in the Personals today, Bess?" she asked. "Have you run across Mr. Right yet?"

Bess giggled. "Not exactly. These ads are the greatest, though. Listen to this guy: 'Sensitive, wealthy executive seeks dream woman to share my exciting life. If you're as perfect as I am, let's talk.' Oh, and here's an athlete for you, George. He *says* all he wants is a tennis partner—oh, no, I take it all back. He's looking for someone in her fifties. And here's one who starts out sounding wonderful—until he mentions the cats."

"What's the problem with that?" George asked. "You like cats."

"I know, but this guy has fifteen of them! It's nice of him to warn us, anyway. No, I guess this won't be the week I fall in love through the Personals."

"Then how about giving the rest of us a chance to read them?" George asked. "I'm done with the sports section."

"Hey, no way! I'm not finished," said Bess. "You're the jock. Nancy's the detective. And it's *my* job to keep us informed about the world of romance." She cast a regretful look at her empty plate and bent her head over the paper again.

For a few minutes the room was silent except for the rustle of newsprint or an occasional hiss when a raindrop fell down the chimney. Finally Bess looked up.

"On the other hand," she said, "here's one that *does* sound interesting. Listen: 'Where are you? I know you're out there. I've been looking for you for two years. If you're blond, blue-eyed, medium-tall, and love to wear white, I must meet you immediately. I have a lot to offer, and I can promise you you won't be sorry. Please, please contact me as soon as possible.'"

Bess put down the paper. "It's me! This guy's looking for me!" she said. "I mean, look at this sweater!" She gestured at the fluffy white mohair sweater she was wearing. "I love to wear white! I'm blond and blue-eyed and medium-tall—boy, this is the first time I've ever been glad I'm not tall. I'm going to answer this ad the minute I get home."

"What are you talking about?" asked George. "You're going to write to a guy who looks for girls in the Personals, just because you happen to own a white sweater? Get serious."

"Oh, you're no fun," said Bess. "So what if I don't wear white all the time? I'm not going to let that stand in the way of a little romance."

"Wearing white's not the point, Bess," Nancy said. "The point is that you know nothing about this man. George is right. You can't go out with a complete stranger just because you answer his description of the perfect girl. He could be a total creep—or worse. Don't waste your time."

"*You're* both being total sticks-in-the-mud," Bess said stubbornly. "Lots of nice people meet other nice people in the Personals. It happens every day. I know this guy isn't a creep. I can just feel it."

Nancy shook her head. Bess had a knack for ignoring what she didn't want to hear. "Well, we can't stop you," she said. "But if you do get in touch with this person, at least promise me you'll meet him in a safe place."

"Come on, Nancy! I'm not a complete baby!" Bess protested. "Okay, I promise. If he wants to get together on a deserted bridge at midnight, I won't go out with him. But I just know nothing like that's going to happen. This time, there's love in the air."

"So that's why it's raining so hard," George muttered. But Bess just smiled.

Nancy didn't have time to wonder whether Bess had called her mystery man. On Monday Ned came home for intersession, and she spent every free minute of that week with him. By the next Sunday night they had seen four movies, shared seven pizzas, and talked on the phone for ten hours.

"My dad always wonders what we find to talk about," she confided to Ned on Sunday night. They were walking home from George's. "He says we spend so much time together when you're home that there can't possibly be anything left to say on the phone. *I* can't explain it to him."

"Well, seeing you in person's even better," Ned said, squeezing her hand. "Especially when there's no case to take you away from me."

"This time I'm all yours, so you'd better appreciate it." They were nearing Nancy's house now. "Want to come in for a little while before you head home?" she asked.

"I'd better not," Ned answered. "I don't know why it is, but my parents want to see me once in a while, too."

"I guess parents are just strange that way." Nancy leaned up to kiss him good night. "I'm so glad you're home," she whispered.

"Me, too. I'll see you tomorrow."

When Ned had vanished from sight, Nancy walked dreamily into the house. It was still early, and she felt restless. There was nothing good on television, and she didn't feel like going to bed. At last she picked up a magazine. She was deep in an article about the dangers of overtanning when the phone rang.

"You might as well get it, Nancy," said her father from his study. "It's not going to be for *me*."

Smiling, Nancy picked up the receiver. "Hi, Ned!" she said happily. "Did you miss me?"

"N-Nancy, is that you?" asked a shaky voice.

"Bess! Sorry, I thought you were Ned. What's up?"

"Oh, Nan, you've got to help me. Remember that Personals ad in the *Record?*"

"The one with all the cats?" Nancy asked. She couldn't wait to hear what was coming.

But Bess sounded as if she were about to burst into tears. "It's—it's not funny. The one I said I was going to answer. Nancy, I *did* answer it. I met the guy tonight. And I think he wants to kill me!"

Chapter

Two

WHAT?" NANCY SAID. "Hang on a minute. Where are you now?"

"I-I'm at home. I just got here. Oh, Nancy, it was the most awful thing! All I could think about was how stupid I'd been! I was so—"

"Bess. Bess," Nancy said patiently. "If you could calm down a little, it would be easier for me to understand what's going on. Now take a deep breath and start at the beginning. Okay?"

But Bess's voice was quavering again. "Nancy, I hate to invite myself over, but would it be all right if I spent the night at your house? No one's home, and it's giving me the creeps being alone here. I promise I'll tell you all about it if you'll just come and get me away from here."

"Where's your car?" Nancy asked.

"No! No! I'm not driving! You know how, in all those scary movies, the heroine gets into her car and there's someone in the back seat, and suddenly she feels hands on her throat, and—"

"All right. All right. I'll come and get you," Nancy said, cutting in. She couldn't tell whether Bess was just being Bess or whether there really was something the matter.

When Nancy rang Bess's bell a few minutes later, there was no answer. A little worried, she rang again—and again. "Bess!" she called, jiggling the door handle. "Are you in there?"

Silence. Then Nancy saw the curtain in the living-room window rustle slightly. In a second the door opened a crack, and Bess peered out nervously. "Are you alone?" she whispered.

"Yes, of course I'm alone!" said Nancy. "Bess, what on earth is the matter with you?"

"I'm sorry. I—I just got scared, that's all. I started to wonder whether anyone had heard me make that call and was just *pretending* to be you at the door."

"Bess Marvin, you're driving me crazy. Now come out, get in the car, and calm down."

"My goodness, girls! What are you doing up so late?" asked Hannah Gruen, the Drews' house-keeper, when Nancy and Bess came in a few

10

minutes later. "Bess! What's happened? You look as though you've seen a ghost."

"I wish that were all I'd seen," Bess said. "Nancy's letting me spend the night here, Hannah. I hope that's all right."

"Of course it is," said Hannah. "I'll go and make up the spare bed now."

"Oh, and do you have any hot chocolate?" Bess asked Nancy in a tiny voice. "I think I deserve some tonight."

"Good idea," Nancy said. "Let's go make a pot."

Over mugs of steaming hot chocolate—Bess's wearing a huge cap of whipped cream—they settled down on the sofa in the living room. "Now," said Nancy, "I want it all. From the beginning."

Bess took a sip and sighed. "Well, the first thing I have to say is that I'll never break a promise to you again."

"That's good to hear. What promise did you break, anyway?" Nancy asked.

"The one where I told you I'd meet that guy from the Personals in a safe, busy place. But let me start at the beginning." Bess took another sip before continuing.

"I wrote him a note with my phone number on it in care of the newspaper. That was last Monday. He must have gotten it right away, because he called me Wednesday night. Nan, he sounded so great! Polite, interesting, cute—"

"You could tell all that over the phone?" Nancy said, interrupting.

"I *thought* so, anyway. We talked for a little while—just about our interests and stuff like that—and then he asked when we could get together. Well, I did remember what you'd said. I suggested the Pizza Palace, but he sounded really disappointed. He said *that* was no place for a first date and that he'd had someplace more romantic in mind. All I could think was how great it was to meet someone who actually used the word 'romantic.' I said okay, and *he* said to meet him at a little restaurant called Bel Canto, at Eightieth and Main, tonight at seven."

Nancy could vaguely remember seeing Bel Canto, a pretty little place on the outskirts of town. "So you said you would?" she asked, prompting Bess.

"Yes. But when I got there, I started to get the creeps. The place was in the middle of nowhere and the parking lot was so dark and deserted that I almost changed my mind right there. Could you pour me another cup of hot chocolate? Thanks.

"So, anyway, I went in, and the restaurant was just about empty. Except that there was one cute guy sitting at a table. He *was* pretty cute," she repeated, as if to herself. "He was blond and blue-eyed too. I went up and introduced myself and sat down."

"What was *his* name?" Nancy asked.

"Oh! Steve. He told me that when I first called

him. Steve Beldon. He gave his phone number in the ad. It's not in the phone book, though—I checked when I got home tonight. So, anyway, I sat down, and the waitress came up to take our orders. He only ordered coffee! At seven at night! I mean, if this was going to be so romantic, you'd think he'd at least have been thinking *dinner*. So that got my suspicions up."

"I should think it would," Nancy said gravely. Bess darted a look at her, then continued her story.

"So I couldn't do anything except order coffee, too, could I? But, Nan, do you know what he said when the waitress had brought the order and gone away?"

"He asked if you took sugar?"

"Nancy!" Bess said indignantly. "Will you get serious? He leaned forward and grabbed my wrist—hard—and said, 'Where's the money?'"

"What money?" Nancy asked, bewildered.

"That's what *I* said, but he just repeated the question. I told him I didn't know what he was talking about. He looked at me for a second, in kind of a creepy way, and then he said, 'All right, if that's the way you want it. But how could you leave the Glove to die? I thought you loved him!'"

"What?"

"And he kept saying it, too," Bess said. "He just kept asking me both questions over and over, in this mean little whisper, until I decided it was time to get out of there. I said, 'Well, thanks for the coffee,' and stood up. I couldn't see the waitress anywhere—she must have been in the back."

Bess's voice was shaky now. "He grabbed my wrist again and just *yanked* me back into my seat. He said he'd be watching me from now on—and that if I made one false move, he'd —he'd kill me! Then he said he was leaving. He told me not to watch him go and not to tell anyone in the restaurant what had happened. Then I had to wait five minutes after he'd left before I got up myself."

Bess looked bleakly at Nancy. "So I did everything he said, and then I drove home and called you—and here I am. Now go ahead and say 'I told you so.'"

"Oh, Bess. What a night you've had," said Nancy, leaning forward and putting her hand on Bess's shoulder. "Especially when you were looking forward to meeting this guy so much."

"Do you think he really is watching me?" Bess asked.

"Oh, no," Nancy said reassuringly. "Not a chance." She knew there was no way to be sure of that, but she didn't want to make Bess even more nervous.

"Well, could you get your father to sue the paper for my mental anguish?" Bess asked. Nancy's father, Carson Drew, was one of the best-known lawyers in River Heights.

Nancy had to laugh. "I'm afraid not. The paper hasn't done anything illegal. They're not responsible for what happens to people who answer their ads." She paused for a moment, thinking.

"All the same, it wouldn't hurt to go by the newspaper offices tomorrow and tell them about this creep. I know that some people who advertise in the Personals are weird, but they're not supposed to be *this* weird. A responsible paper would want to know about this guy.

"Now let's get some sleep," she continued. "And the first thing in the morning we'll go over and talk to the person at the paper in charge of these ads."

"Yeah," Bess said more cheerfully. "We'll tell them it's just not acceptable to ruin my life like this."

"You do the talking, Nancy," Bess said nervously the next day. The two girls had just gotten out of Nancy's Mustang in the visitors' parking lot at the *Morning Record.*

"No problem," Nancy answered. Then she stopped for a minute and looked at the building. She knew it all too well—one of her most important cases had involved a *Record* reporter. Just standing there brought back a flood of memories.

The building looked ordinary enough. Its right side was covered with scaffolding, though, and a few workmen were sandblasting the facade.

Nancy glanced quickly at Bess. "What's the matter?" Bess asked.

"Nothing," Nancy said, pulling herself together. "Let's go."

She began walking briskly toward the main entrance, Bess following a couple of paces behind.

Just as the girls were about to walk through the door, there was an ominous rumbling sound. Then a brick crashed to the ground right next to Nancy's foot. Startled, she glanced up.

A huge, dark shape teetered precariously on the edge of the scaffolding overhead. It blocked out the sun as it hurtled down.

Nancy gasped. A cartload of bricks was falling straight at them!

Chapter

Three

Iᴛ ᴀʟʟ ʜᴀᴘᴘᴇɴᴇᴅ in seconds.

Bess screamed. Instantly Nancy grabbed her arm and yanked her backward so fast that both girls fell to the ground. Before they could scramble to their feet, an avalanche of bricks had crashed to the sidewalk inches in front of them. Then there was silence. The two girls watched, dazed, as the dust settled.

"Are you all right?" A man rushed up to them and helped them to their feet. "That was unbelievable! I was behind you and could see it about to happen, but there was no way to get to you in time."

"I think we're okay," Nancy said. "Bess?" She

turned to her friend, and Bess nodded. "Did you see what happened?" Nancy asked the man. "Was there anyone up there?"

"Not that I saw," he said. "The cart just toppled over and the bricks came shooting down. Maybe they hadn't been loaded right."

"It still seems strange—" Nancy glanced up at the scaffolding. If there had been anyone there, he certainly wasn't there now. "Well, you must be right," she said. "Anyway, thanks for checking on us. I guess we were just lucky this time."

"Guess so. Lucky no one else was here, too." The man walked away, and Bess turned to Nancy.

"You see?" she said. "He's still trying to get me!"

"Oh, come on, Bess," answered Nancy. "I'm sure it was just a coincidence. Not a very nice one, I admit, but what else could it have been? If this guy wanted to get you, there are lots of easier ways to do it." She hoped she was right. "Anyway, let's go in and tell them about him."

"Well, *I* think dumping a load of bricks on a girl would be a *very* easy way to get rid of her," grumbled Bess as she followed Nancy through the double doors of the *Record* building.

"May I help you?" asked a businesslike receptionist as the girls walked inside.

"I hope so," Nancy answered, smiling. "We need to speak to whoever is in charge of your Personals."

"Do you wish to place an ad?"

"Not exactly," said Nancy.

"May I inquire as to the purpose of your visit?" the receptionist asked silkily.

"We need to make a complaint," blurted out Bess before Nancy could say anything.

The receptionist sighed. "All right. Go up to Lena Verle on the fifth floor."

"Lena Verle? Doesn't she sound mean?" said Bess as they walked toward the elevator.

"Well, maybe she's nicer than she sounds," Nancy answered.

But she wasn't. The fifth floor was a hive of computer terminals. When they asked the nearest man which one belonged to Lena Verle, his face clouded for a second.

"She's over there, in the corner," he said. "And I hope for your sakes that it's urgent."

Hunched over the terminal in the corner was a young woman dressed in the drabbest clothes Nancy had ever seen—a droopy olive green cardigan, a limp beige blouse, and a shapeless gray skirt. She looked up irritably as they approached.

"Ms. Verle?" Nancy asked. "I wonder if we could talk to you for a minute."

"Well, go ahead—talk," said Lena Verle.

"It's about something private. Is there someplace we could be alone? This will only take a little while."

"Look, I'm not a real editor," said Lena. *"I*

don't have an office of my own. We can talk here or out in the hall. It's up to you."

"The hall would be fine," Nancy said politely.

Ms. Verle stood up without a word and swept past them to the hallway—where she sat in a chair next to the elevator. It was the only chair.

Nancy didn't waste any time. "My friend here had a pretty unpleasant experience when she contacted one of the people whose ads you ran in your Personals column. We thought you might know who it was." She held up the cut-out ad. Lena Verle's eyes flicked over the paragraph, but she made no move to take it.

"How should I know?" she answered tersely. "It could have been placed by anyone. I don't keep track of the people who come in here."

"Are the ads placed in person or by mail?" asked Nancy.

"Both," snapped Ms. Verle.

"Maybe you could check your files to see if this one was mailed," suggested Nancy. "We'd like to trace this person if we possibly can. He made some very unpleasant threats."

"I'm sorry," said Ms. Verle, who didn't sound sorry at all, "but that would violate confidentiality. And of course you realize I can't possibly do that."

"But the guy threatened to kill me!" protested Bess. "You can't keep a person like *that* confidential!"

"Look," said Ms. Verle rapidly, "I'm not responsible for people who are desperate enough to answer these ads. I'm not paid to baby-sit people like you. It's your own fault if—"

"But don't you think it's important for us to find this guy?" Nancy asked. "We wouldn't have to bother you—we'd just like to take a look at your records."

"No!" Lena cried.

"We'll let ourselves out, Ms. Verle. Thank you so much for your time," Nancy replied testily. She reached over and hit the elevator button with a decisive click.

"I knew as soon as I saw her that she wouldn't be any help," Nancy said when the doors had closed. "But I kept hoping my hunch was wrong."

Bess was still sputtering. "I can't believe that woman!" she fumed. "I bet she knows *exactly* who placed that ad. Well, I'm going to figure out some way to make her talk."

"It's not worth it," Nancy said soothingly. "We'll find our man without the help of Lena Verle."

"Nancy, there is no way I can forget about a woman who called me desperate. And we still don't know how to track down that guy."

"That's certainly true for now." Nancy paused, thinking. "Look, I know some people who work here. I think our best bet would be to talk to the editor in chief. His name is Hank Whittaker. Since we're on our way down to the

lobby anyway, let's just check with the receptionist to see if he's in his office."

But he wasn't. He was on vacation and not
expected back for a week. "He did stop in briefly
on his way to the airport this morning, but I
guess you just missed him," said the receptionist.

"Well, who else can we talk to?" Bess asked
Nancy.

Nancy furrowed her brows. "There are a few
reporters, and maybe a couple of editors—but I
don't think any of them would be as helpful as
Mr. Whittaker," she said. "I really think our best
bet is to wait for him to come back. And for now,
you should try to put all of this out of your
mind."

"Put that guy out of my mind? When he tried
to kill me?" Bess shrieked.

"Well, that's more pleasant than thinking
about the creep, isn't it?" Nancy replied.

"You have a point," Bess said. "So let's go get
some ice cream. That should help me forget."

After she had taken Bess home, Nancy drove
out to the Bel Canto restaurant. Perhaps she'd be
able to find a lead there. At the restaurant she
asked to speak to the waitress who'd been on
duty the night before.

"Sure, I noticed that couple," the waitress told
her. "I always notice couples who fight in public.
She seemed nice, and he seemed like a real
crank."

"You didn't try to stop him? This was a little more than a fight," Nancy told her.

"To tell you the truth, I was embarrassed. I would have felt really stupid trying to break up a lovers' quarrel—and they were talking so quietly there was no way to tell that anything else was going on. I knew that if it got noisy I'd have to step in, but until it did, I just kept out of the way."

"And nobody else in the restaurant noticed?"

"They weren't talking loudly enough for anyone to notice. Besides, it was Sunday night. It's real slow for us."

"So you didn't see when he left?" Nancy asked.

"No, I really didn't. Is your friend all right? You're making me feel terrible!"

"She's fine—and I guess you couldn't have known." Nancy sighed. "But could you do me a favor? If you ever see the guy again, would you give me a call? Here's my number."

The waitress promised to call, but Nancy knew there wasn't much chance that he would ever come back.

It wasn't until the following Sunday that Nancy talked to Bess again. She was giving herself a manicure when Hannah poked her head into her bedroom.

"Nancy, Bess is here to see you. She seems a little upset."

"Uh-oh." Nancy waved her left hand, trying to dry the polish. "Could you tell her to come up, Hannah? If I move, I know I'll bash my hand against something before my nails are dry."

She heard Bess thumping up the stairs before bursting into the room.

"Have you seen this?" Bess demanded, holding out the Sunday paper.

Nancy took it gingerly, but when she read what Bess was pointing to she forgot all about her nails. In the Personals column was the same ad Bess had seen two weeks before. It was identical to the earlier one—except that it had a new last line.

"You'd better find me before I find you!"

Chapter

Four

"W OW," NANCY SAID, putting the paper down. "This is more serious than I thought."

Bess looked totally panic-stricken. Nancy gave Bess a little pat on the shoulder. "We'll find this character," she said consolingly. "I promise you. I'll be talking to Mr. Whittaker tomorrow, and I'm sure he'll be helpful. The case will be wrapped up before you know it."

Bess exhaled shakily. "Well, I certainly hope you're right. And try to get him to fire that horrible Lena Verle while you're at it."

The next morning Nancy put on a khaki skirt, navy blazer, and white blouse with a floppy tie—what Ned always called her "future executive of America outfit." No matter how many cases she had handled, it was always awkward telling complete strangers that she was about to investigate them, and she wanted to look as professional as possible.

The ultra-efficient receptionist at the *Record* was no more helpful than before. "I'm sorry, but you won't be able to see Mr. Whittaker without an appointment," she told Nancy, without looking up.

"Then I'd like to make an appointment," Nancy answered pleasantly.

"I don't make his appointments. His secretary would have to do that for you."

"Then I'll go up and see *her*. Which floor, please?"

"The sixth, but you can't go up to the executive floor without a visitor's pass."

"Can you please give me a visitor's pass, then?"

"How can I, when you don't have an appointment?"

Nancy saw this conversation was going nowhere. She would have to take matters into her own hands.

"Well then, I guess I'll just have to forget about seeing Mr. Whittaker," she said demurely. The receptionist looked up and smiled tightly. Nancy walked to the elevators. When she was inside one, she calmly pushed the button for the sixth floor.

She exited the elevator. Here there were no computer terminals—just offices—and Nancy marched by each one until she found the plaque reading Hank Whittaker, Editor in Chief. There was no secretary to be seen. Nancy rapped smartly on the door, and when a pleasant-looking young man answered it—Nancy always found it hard to believe he was in charge—she swept right into her prepared speech.

"Mr. Whittaker? I don't know if you remember me. We met very briefly a few months ago. My name is Nancy Drew, and I'm a private detective. I'd like to talk to you about your Personals column. A friend of mine received some very nasty threats from a man whose ad your paper ran, and I have reason to think he may be following her still. With your permission, I'd like—"

"Nancy Drew, you say?" Mr. Whittaker said, interrupting her suddenly. "Are you the same girl who investigated the Ann Granger case?"

Ann Granger had been a reporter on his newspaper. Although she now worked for a Chicago paper, she and the Drews were still close friends. Ann had uncovered a citywide scandal in which Nancy's father had been framed.

"I—yes, I am," Nancy answered, startled.

"Then everyone at the paper is in your debt," said Mr. Whittaker, shaking her hand warmly. "Ann's a fine reporter, and I know how grateful she was when you helped her out."

27

"And I'm grateful to her for helping to clear my father's name," Nancy said. "I'm sorry that my business here today is less pleasant, but—"

"Come right in and sit down." Mr. Whittaker interrupted her again. When she was settled, he said, "Now, start again."

Nancy did, and he listened closely. "Well, I'm not sure if we'll be able to provide you with the identity of the person who placed that ad."

"Because it's confidential?"

"No, not because of that. It's just that *we* may not know who he is. If he paid by check, that's one thing—but if he paid with cash, we'll have a lot more trouble tracking him down."

"I see," Nancy said.

"But if you'd like to spend a couple of days checking out the Personals column, be my guest," Mr. Whittaker said. "Maybe this creep will take out another ad. You helped *us* out once, and it would be a pleasure to do the same for you. Besides, it's to our advantage to have this all cleared up as soon as possible."

"Thank you. I was hoping you'd feel that way," said Nancy, relieved. "I wonder—I'd like to keep this as quiet as possible for now. Do you think you could try not to—"

"I won't say anything to the staff. Don't worry. Of course, I'm not closely involved with the day-to-day work on the Personals column," Mr. Whittaker added. "But you can work as closely as you need to with our Personals editor, Lena

Verle. I guess we'll have to tell *her* what you're up to, but I'll ask her to keep it to herself."

Nancy's heart sank. She'd been hoping she wouldn't have to deal with Lena Verle again, but obviously avoiding the woman was going to be impossible. "Actually, I met Ms. Verle yesterday," she said. "She—she wasn't sure there was any way to figure out who'd placed the ad." Nancy didn't want to say how unpleasant she found Ms. Verle.

"Oh, I'm sure she'll be helpful," said Mr. Whittaker heartily. "Come on. I'll just bring you down to her pod—that's what we call the cubicles around here—and fill her in."

Lena Verle didn't look too thrilled when the two of them walked up, but at least she didn't say anything nasty.

"She can work hand in hand with you, Lena," Mr. Whittaker said, finishing up. "Why don't you give her a little tour around the place now? Ms. Drew, it's nice to have you aboard, even under these circumstances. If I can be of any help, just let me know." With a cheery wave he left Nancy and Lena alone.

There was a little silence after he had gone. "Look, I know this isn't going to be much fun for you," Nancy finally said. "I'll try not to get in your way, and maybe I can even help you out a little once I know the ropes."

"I doubt it," Lena said listlessly. "He wanted me to show you around—should I do it now?"

"Please." Nancy was determined to keep things pleasant.

Nancy wasn't sure what she'd been expecting, but the *Record*'s offices looked pretty much like most modern offices. Besides Lena's floor—the newsroom—where the writers had cubicles, and the floor above where the executives were, there was a floor for the paper's business staff. Another floor contained the file rooms and library, and the building's first two floors were taken up with printing equipment. There was a locked room filled with huge, quietly humming computers in addition to a mailroom and a small kitchen filled with what seemed to be thousands of discarded coffee cups. *Please* keep this room clean! advised a tattered sign above the grimy sink.

What distinguished the offices as those of a newspaper was the noise level—at least in the newsroom. Telephones rang constantly; reporters talked at the tops of their voices; and the wire-service machines clattered away. This, to Nancy, seemed like what a typical newspaper should sound like.

"Any questions?" Lena asked.

"Where's all the cigarette smoke and the guys yelling 'Copy'?" Nancy asked, smiling.

Lena Verle looked at her humorlessly. "That's only in the movies," she said. "We don't need copyboys now that everything's computerized. And hardly anyone smokes anymore."

Before Nancy could respond, a woman in her

early twenties rushed up to them. "A new face!" she said to Nancy. "Is this your first day?"

"This is Nancy Drew. She's a—" Lena Verle began.

Nancy cut her off. "I'm going to be working with Lena for the next couple of days, but I'm not on staff," she said.

"Too bad. We could use some new blood around here. By the way, my name's Lucy Price. I write for the Home section. Do you know any celebrities? I've got to write a piece about celebrity bathrooms, and none of the celebrities' agents I've called will let me interview them. I'm already down to the *B* list, and the article's due in two days. You're not famous, by any chance?"

Nancy smiled. "Not exactly."

"Well, let me know if you think of anyone —that's my phone! Maybe a star is returning my call! See you around, Nancy." And she rushed off to her desk.

It made Nancy a little uncomfortable that Lucy hadn't even said hello to Lena Verle. She turned back to the silent woman next to her. "Well, thanks for giving me the tour," she said. "If you have time, I'd love to hear a little about how your job works."

"I've got time," Lena said curtly. "Come back to my desk."

As it turned out, Lena's job was fairly simple. Personal ads that were placed in person were left downstairs with the receptionist. More often, the ads were mailed in. Each "advertiser" was assigned a box number, and people who answered the ad mailed their responses to the box numbers.

"They never phone in?" Nancy asked.

"No," Lena said impatiently. "Sometimes they try, but I cut them off. It would take forever if everyone phoned in their responses."

"So you'd never see anyone who placed an ad in person?" Nancy asked.

"That's right."

Nancy sighed. That meant she'd have to talk to the receptionist downstairs, the same one who tried to keep her from seeing Mr. Whittaker. Between the receptionist and Lena, she was going to be having some pretty grim conversations.

"I'd like to look at the ads that have come in for this week," she said. "But I guess I'll do that tomorrow. Thanks for your help, Lena. I'll go and say goodbye to Mr. Whittaker, and then try to talk to the receptionist. I'll see you tomorrow."

Lena had already turned back to her computer, and she didn't answer.

"You settling in okay?" Mr. Whittaker boomed out when Nancy peeked in at his door.

"Just fine," she said. "I was wondering if I could have a note from you to take to the receptionist downstairs. I'd like to ask her a few questions, and I think she'll be more likely to answer if she knows you've okayed it."

"I'll make it even easier than that," Mr. Whittaker answered, picking up the phone and dialing. "I'll just call her right now. Hello, Dawn? Listen, a very nice girl named Nancy Drew is about to come downstairs to ask you a few questions. You go ahead and answer her, and don't worry too much about correct office procedure.

"That ought to do it," he said, hanging up.

"Thanks a lot, Mr. Whittaker," Nancy said. "I'll see you tomorrow."

Dawn was a lot more helpful than she had been that morning. As helpful as she could be, anyway, considering that no ads had been placed in person for the past three weeks. She hadn't noticed anything about the guy who'd placed Bess's ad because there hadn't been anything to see. As Nancy walked out of the *Record* building toward the parking lot, she was beginning to wonder if this case would ever go anywhere.

She was thinking so hard that she didn't notice the hunched figure leaning against her car until she was about to open the door. It was Lena Verle.

"I just talked to the guy who placed that ad!" she gasped. "He said to tell you that you'll die if you investigate this case!"

Chapter
Five

I RAN OUT here to warn you," Lena went on as Nancy stared at her. "I'm glad I caught you in time. He sounds like a real monster." Lena was so animated that she seemed like a different person.

"What did he say? Could you start at the beginning?" Nancy asked, speaking calmly. She could hardly believe the man could have caught up with her so fast.

"There's not much to tell, really," Lena said. "Right after you'd left, I got a phone call from a guy asking for you. When I said you'd gone for the day, he got pretty angry. He asked for your home phone number, and when I told him I didn't have it, he started swearing and—and told me what I just told you, that you'll die if you investigate this any further."

"It seems unbelievable," Nancy said. "I can't think of a single way he could have found out about me. Unless—"

She was thinking aloud now, and Lena was watching her closely. "Unless Mr. Whittaker had accidentally told him. But that's impossible! No, I can't believe it's Mr. Whittaker," she continued. "But he's the only person I told besides—" Suddenly Nancy caught her breath. "Dawn! She must have put the call through. I'm going right back in there to talk to her."

"Oh, I wouldn't bother," Lena said nervously. "I'm sure Dawn didn't—"

Nancy was already striding across the parking lot. After a second, Lena followed her.

"I still don't think you should—" Lena was protesting as Nancy strode through the double doors into the lobby.

"Lena Verle just got a threatening call from the man I'm looking for," she said. "It would have been about five minutes ago. Did you notice anything about the voice of the guy who called her?"

Dawn looked bewildered. "No one's called here in the last five minutes," she said. "She hasn't had any calls so far today."

"Maybe he called on my direct line," Lena put in quickly.

"But you don't *have* a—" Dawn said as Lena spoke again.

"What about your friend, Nancy?" she said. *"She* knew about this. Maybe she called this guy and told him what was going on."

"You mean Bess? That's ridiculous," Nancy said. "Bess is terrified of the man!"

"That's what she says," Lena answered.

"What?" Nancy said incredulously.

"Anyway, isn't this all beside the point?" Lena went on. "It doesn't matter how this guy found out about you. Your life is in danger, Nancy! You're not going to investigate any further, are you?"

"Of course I am!" Nancy answered.

"But you can't!"

Wait a minute, Nancy thought to herself. Why is Lena suddenly so concerned for my safety? "You sound as though you want me to stop investigating," she said thoughtfully.

"Oh, no, it's not that! It's just that when I realized that you might actually get killed, I guess I—well, worried about you. And you *will* stop, won't you?"

There was a pause.

"Won't you?" Lena repeated.

"The timing," Nancy said slowly. "The timing *is* too convenient. You say you got this call right after I'd left?"

"That's—that's right."

"And you have a direct line, you say?"

36

"No, she doesn't," said Dawn. "Not unless they've put one in for her today. Can somebody please tell me what's going on here?"

"I think maybe Lena can," said Nancy, but Lena had just bolted outside through the main door.

"Dawn, I'll fill you in later," Nancy said grimly. "But it'll have to wait until I get this straightened out."

Lena had a head start across the parking lot, but Nancy was quicker. In a matter of seconds she had caught up with Lena and grabbed her shoulder.

"All right, tell *me* what's going on," Nancy said. "And I want the facts this time, please."

There were tears in Lena's eyes when she turned to face Nancy.

"You're going to get me fired, aren't you?" she cried. "You think it's my fault this all happened!"

"Nobody's trying to get anyone fired," Nancy said more gently.

"Yes, you are! You'll tell Mr. Whittaker it's because of me that that guy's ad ran in the paper! But I don't know who he was! I was just doing my job! Please, you've got to stop your investigation! Everyone hates me, and I need this job so badly!" Tears were running down her face now.

"You pretended you'd gotten the call so I'd go away and leave you alone?" Nancy asked.

"Of course I did! What would *you* have done?"

"But, Lena, I don't think you're responsible for what's happened," said Nancy sympathetically. "I'm not trying to get you in trouble —really, I'm not. I just want to stop this guy before he hurts anyone. Okay?"

Lena sniffed. "Do you promise?"

"I promise. Besides, Mr. Whittaker spoke very highly of you. Don't you realize that if you help with the investigation you'll look even better on the job?"

Lena was silent for a minute. "I guess you're right," she said at last.

"As far as everyone hating you—well, perhaps you should try to be more friendly and get to know people."

Lena looked away. "It's just that I'm so worried all the time. I'm afraid someone will notice what a bad job I'm doing."

"Why do you think you're doing a bad job? You seem to me to be doing a good job," Nancy said warmly. "Come on, I'll walk back to the building with you."

Then she heard a familiar voice. "Nancy!" She turned to see Ned jogging toward her.

"I stopped by your house, and Hannah told me you were here. I just thought I'd come by and see if you had time to—oh, am I interrupting something?" he said as he caught sight of Lena's tear-stained face.

"Not at all," Nancy said. "We were just heading back to the paper for a minute. I'll be free to leave then. This is Lena Verle, by the way. She's going to be helping me with the investigation."

As the three of them continued to walk across the parking lot, Ned stopped suddenly. "Stone in my shoe," he said, and bent down to take it out.

At that moment they heard the roar of a car as it moved toward them. Nancy glanced up—and gasped.

A dark blue car was heading straight at her. Nancy jumped out of the way, pulling Lena with her.

"Ned!" she shouted. "Look out!"

But the car hit Ned full force, hurling him high into the air, and sped away before he hit the ground with a terrible thud.

Chapter

Six

FOR A HORRIBLE moment everything stood still, and then Nancy dashed toward Ned. "Get the license-plate number!" she said over her shoulder to Lena.

Ned was lying on his back, his head bent at a sickeningly sharp angle. His mouth was half open. His face was gray, and it felt clammy when Nancy touched it. He was absolutely still.

Oh, no, no! Please let him be alive, she thought frantically to herself as she felt his neck for a pulse. She almost sobbed with relief when she realized his heart was still beating. His pulse was shallow and rapid, though. He'd gone into shock.

Nancy didn't dare try to move him, in case

40

he'd hurt his spine. The only thing she could do was to make him as comfortable as possible. "Oh, where's Lena?" she moaned as she raced toward her car.

There was a blanket in the trunk. She put it there only a few weeks before when she'd been planning a picnic, and now she breathed a silent prayer for having forgotten to take it out. She ran back and placed it gently over Ned.

Should she put something under his feet to elevate them? she wondered, and then realized that he might have hurt his head. If he had, raising his feet would do more harm than good.

Nancy looked around. Should she leave Ned alone and go for help? She'd have to, if—oh, there was Lena rushing back at last.

"Nancy!" Lena was panting and apologetic. "He—he got away. I couldn't read the plate number. My glasses are back at the—"

"Go in and call an ambulance!" Nancy said, interrupting her. "I'll wait here."

"Shouldn't we put a pillow under his head?" Lena asked. "My jacket—"

"No!" Nancy said emphatically. "It might hurt his neck. Just go!"

Lena rushed toward the *Record* building without a backward glance, and Nancy was left alone to wait.

She sat down on the cold asphalt and buried her face in her hands. "Oh, Ned," she whispered. "I'm so, so sorry." It nearly broke her heart to see him in his present condition, and she yearned for the ambulance to come.

Nancy was sure the accident hadn't really been an accident. The driver of that car had meant to hit someone—her. Poor Ned had been at the wrong place at the exact wrong time.

Would he die?

She couldn't let herself think about that. Nancy glanced at her watch. She had probably been sitting there for only a couple of minutes. Depending on traffic, it would take at least five minutes for an ambulance to reach them.

Another minute passed, and Mr. Whittaker, looking solid and reassuring to Nancy, came running toward her. "Lena said to tell you they're on their way," he said. "She called me right after she'd called the ambulance. She wanted to come back out with me, but I told her to sit tight—no sense in having the whole staff out here. Is that the ambulance?"

It was. Its wail was cut short abruptly as it swooped toward them. Two white-jacketed paramedics jumped out and instantly began checking Ned's vital signs. "Pulse is thready," one murmured to the other. "He's in shock."

Just as quickly they checked to see whether any bones were broken. "Looks okay, but I'm worried about the head. Better radio them what we're bringing in." They slid a stiffened piece of canvas under Ned, eased him onto a stretcher, and lifted him into the back of the ambulance.

"You were with him when it happened?" one of the men asked Nancy.

"Yes," she answered in a distracted voice. She was trying to watch what was going on in the ambulance.

"You want to ride to the hospital with him?"

"No, I'd better take my own car."

"All right. Let's go." He jumped back into the ambulance.

"Which hospital?" Nancy called.

"Highland Memorial," the paramedic shouted back. Then the ambulance shot out onto the road. The shriek of the siren flew back to them as the car vanished from sight.

"Goodbye. I've got to get over there," Nancy told Mr. Whittaker. "I guess I'll see you tomorrow, depending on how he is." At that moment, the investigation seemed like some kind of faraway dream.

"You look upset," said Mr. Whittaker. "Wouldn't you like to come into the building and get a hot drink or something before you go?"

"No. No, I can't, but thanks anyway," she answered. "I've got to get over there as fast as I can!"

Mr. Whittaker patted her on the shoulder. "He'll be fine," he said. "Let me know if there's anything I can do."

"I will." Nancy turned on her heel and ran for her car.

* * *

Two exhausting hours passed. Nancy's eyes hurt from the glare of the fluorescent lights in the emergency room's waiting area. Three cups of black coffee on an empty stomach were making her feel even more jittery than before.

The time crawled since Ned had been taken in to be examined. Nancy had tried to call his parents, but they weren't at home. She'd called her house to let her father know she wouldn't be home for dinner. She filled a nurse in on what had happened, and then she waited. And waited.

Across the hall from the waiting room Nancy could see the nurses' station. Twice she had gone to ask if there was any news. The second time, the nurse had obviously been so frazzled that Nancy didn't dare ask again. The activity in the waiting room only made things worse. Babies were squalling; an enormous woman across from Nancy was crying softly, a father and son were having an argument about whose fault the accident that had brought them there had been. On top of everything else, the room was infuriatingly hot.

Nancy closed her eyes and leaned back in her molded plastic chair. She kept thinking about Ned's parents. What was she going to say when she finally reached them? "I'm sorry, but Ned's in the hospital because of my job." "Your son's been hurt because he stopped by to see me." She knew she was blaming herself more than Ned's parents would, but she couldn't help it. She loved

Ned and he was badly hurt. She prayed for good news from the doctors.

"Miss Drew?" She opened her eyes again. A man in a white coat was leaning into the waiting room. "Could I have a word with you?" he asked.

"You still haven't reached the boy's parents?" he asked when they were outside. She shook her head. "Then I'll fill you in on what's happening.

"Fortunately there are no internal injuries." Nancy sighed with relief. The car had hit Ned so hard that she knew internal injuries had been a very real possibility. "But he does have some head injuries, though we're still not sure about their extent. We're waiting for the X rays now. I think you might as well go home for tonight. We won't have the results for a while."

Nancy cleared her throat. "All right. Can I say goodbye to him before I go, or will that be too much of a—too much of a strain for him?"

"I'm sorry," the doctor answered kindly. "I didn't make myself clear. Mr. Nickerson hasn't regained consciousness yet."

"He's still unconscious?" Nancy whispered. "How long will that last?"

"We can't really predict, Ms. Drew. It could be twenty-four hours before he comes to."

"Twenty-four hours?"

"The length of time doesn't necessarily mean anything," the doctor added hastily. "Of course we'll do a CAT scan if he isn't conscious by then. But that's a very remote possibility.

"I do think you ought to go home and get some rest," he said again. "You're not doing either of you any good by waiting around. Not when he doesn't even know you're here."

Wearily Nancy pushed open the front door of her house. She walked into the living room and threw herself down on the sofa, too tired even to call out that she was home.

But her father had heard her come in, and he came running in from his study. "How is he?" he asked.

"Terrible," Nancy said bluntly. It was all she could do to keep her composure as she filled her father in. "I've just come from his house. I went over there after I left the hospital and waited in the driveway until they came home."

Nancy shuddered. "Oh, Dad, I hope I never have to do anything like that again! They'd just come home from a party. They were so happy to see me—" Her voice broke, and she threw herself into her father's arms.

"Are they at the hospital now?" her father asked.

"Yes. They jumped back into the car and drove away without even saying goodbye," Nancy said. She looked as forlorn as her father had ever seen her.

"You've had a terrible day, and I think you should go right up to bed and sort things out in the morning," said Mr. Drew. "A good night's sleep will—"

Just then the telephone rang. Nancy jumped nervously, but she heard Hannah hang up almost instantly. Then Hannah came into the room, her face strained and anxious.

"They hung up again," she said. "It's been happening all evening. I keep thinking it'll be news of Ned, but all I hear is a click and the dial tone."

"Oh, no!" Nancy whispered. With everything that had happened, she completely forgot the case she was working on. Was the caller somehow connected with her investigation?

"What's the matter, Nancy?" her father asked. "I mean, what *else* is the matter?"

"I'm just wondering if—"

The telephone rang again. Nancy took a deep breath. Then she strode into the hall and picked up the receiver.

"Nancy Drew here," she said crisply.

Silence—and then a husky voice. Nancy couldn't tell if it was a man or a woman.

"Just think of this afternoon as a little warning," the voice said. "And stay out of my way from now on!"

Chapter

Seven

"Nancy, what's the matter?" asked Carson Drew, who had followed her into the hall. "Is it something about Ned?"

Nancy shook her head. "No. It's my case," she said. "Somehow the guy who's been threatening Bess is on to me. He's the one who crashed into Ned, and now he's after me. The thing I don't understand is how he knows who I am or that I'm trying to track him down."

"He wants you to drop the case?" her father asked.

"Yes. But now that Ned's been hurt, there's no way I'm going to give up until I see this would-be murderer brought to justice."

Her father bit his lip. "Nan, I know we have this talk about once a month," he said. "And I know you won't quit a case just because it's dangerous. But it seems to me that you may be too emotionally involved. Couldn't you turn this one over to the pros?"

"Dad, I can't quit—you know that," she said quietly but firmly.

Carson Drew sighed. "All right. I can't talk you out of this, but let me warn you about one thing—"

"I *know* the case is dangerous," Nancy said.

"No. What I was going to say is that you're going to have to be especially careful on this case. You're doing it for personal reasons, not professional ones. So you'll have to make sure your emotions don't get in the way of your judgment." He smiled at her. "Okay?"

"Okay," she answered.

"So go to bed!" her father said. "Things really will look better in the morning, honey."

"I hope so." Nancy kissed him good night and dragged herself up the stairs.

It was hours before she could sleep. Every time she'd doze off, a vision of the car zooming toward Ned would jar her awake, and she'd find herself sitting bolt upright in her bed, her heart hammering in her chest.

The birds had started singing when Nancy finally fell asleep, and the harsh buzz of her alarm clock woke her with a start. Groaning, she sat up and squinted at the clock through eyelids that felt as if they were lined with sandpaper. Seven-thirty. Her head was throbbing.

Nancy flopped back down onto the pillow, hiding her face in the crook of her arm. After a second, though, she forced herself to sit up. She wasn't going to be good for much that day if she couldn't even get up on time.

"Feeling any better?" Hannah asked her after she went downstairs.

Nancy grimaced. "Well, the shower helped some. No, I don't want any breakfast, Hannah —just some coffee. I have to get over to the hospital."

"Better call first," Hannah advised. "There's no sense in making a trip if they're not going to let you see him."

"Good point." Nancy's hand was shaking a little as she dialed the number, but when she hung up she looked like a new person.

"He's awake! He's doing fine!" she caroled, catching Hannah by the waist and whirling her around the kitchen. "His parents are with him now, but the nurse said it'll be all right if I stop by in about an hour. Oh, I can't believe it! May I change my mind about breakfast, Hannah? Suddenly I'm famished."

"Ned?" Nancy peeked timidly around the door of his hospital room. "Are you awake?"

"Nancy! I've been waiting for you!" Ned's voice was a feeble imitation of itself. "Come on in. Sorry I can't get up."

Nancy's face fell when she saw him. He was very pale, and his eyes glowed with a feverish brightness. She couldn't help feeling that the boy lying in the bed wasn't Ned at all. *Her* Ned had been replaced by a total stranger.

But Ned was looking worried now. It must be all too obvious what she was thinking. Nancy cleared her throat. "Nice outfit," she said lightly, pointing at his green hospital gown. "Is that the best the hospital has to offer?" She crossed the room to kiss him.

"Afraid so. Hey, don't look so scared," he whispered, clutching her hand. "I'm okay. Really. I have a concussion. It could be a lot worse."

"Oh, Ned . . ." For a second Nancy couldn't speak. "I—when that car hit you, I thought . . ."

"I'm *fine.*" Ned's voice was stronger now. "I only wish I could prove it to you. But I guess that'll have to wait a couple of days."

"I love you so much," Nancy said. "Do you *promise* you're not mad at me for getting you into this?"

"Mad at you? Nancy, if that car had hit you, I'd never have forgiven myself."

Nancy smiled wryly. "Well, now you know how I feel."

"Nancy, no one's mad at you. My parents are

51

just glad I'm okay. Now calm down and give me a kiss."

When Nancy lifted her head, she looked a lot happier. "Okay, I'll take your word for everything," she said.

"That's good." But suddenly Ned gasped. "Don't worry, it's—it's— It just hurts a little," he muttered. "They can't give me any painkillers." His teeth were clenched. "I'm sorry, it makes it a little hard to—"

"Ms. Drew?" It was Dr. Meinhold, the same physician who'd spoken to Nancy the night before. "I think it's time for Ned to get some rest."

"Of course." Nancy bent down and kissed Ned again. "Stay away from the nurses, now," she said as cheerfully as she could.

Ned's eyes were squeezed tightly shut. He opened them to give her a quick smile, gripped her hand for a second, and turned his head away. With a lump in her throat Nancy followed Dr. Meinhold out the door.

"Don't worry if Ned seems to—well, to come unplugged over the next few days," the doctor said when they were out in the hall. "He's in a lot of pain."

"Can't you give him something to make him feel better? It's horrible to watch him suffer like that."

"We can't, Ms. Drew. We're still concerned about his head injury. No drugs until we're sure his brain's really recovering—medication might suppress new symptoms. I know it's hard to watch, but it's really best for him.

"I gathered from what Ned's parents said that you're some kind of detective?" Dr. Meinhold asked.

"Yes, I am. I was working on a case yesterday when Ned was—when that car hit him."

"I see. I do think it would be best if you avoided talking about your work with him until he's feeling a little stronger. He'll recover faster if we can keep him from getting worried. Will that be too much of a problem?"

"Oh, no," Nancy said. "I'll just—I'll just talk about other things."

Then she gathered all her courage and asked the question that had been bothering her the most. "Dr. Meinhold, will Ned still be able to go out for sports when he's recovered?"

She held her breath during the silence that followed. "All we can do is—wait and see," Dr. Meinhold said at last.

"How is he?" Lena Verle asked eagerly.

Getting back into her car and driving to the *Record* had been one of the hardest things Nancy had ever done. Her every thought, every emotion was centered on Ned, and she just wanted to sit in the hospital beside him. Now that she was at the paper, though, she didn't want to talk about him—even to Lena.

"He's doing pretty well, considering," she

said. "But—I hope you'll understand—I just can't talk about it now. If you can give me some kind of work to do, I'll feel much better."

Lena looked a little disappointed, but she produced a stack of letters cheerfully enough.

"I thought you might want to look through these," she said. "They're the letters we'll be running this week. I don't know if there's anything suspicious about any of them, but you'll get a good laugh from some of them, anyway."

"This is perfect," Nancy said, brightening. "It's just what I need. I've never been involved with a case where it was okay to read other people's mail!"

There was every kind of letter imaginable in the stack, from utterly prim to the complete opposite. Some had been neatly typed on business stationery. A couple were handwritten so crudely that Nancy was sure the writers had been trying to disguise their script—which was kind of silly, she thought, since no one was forcing them to use their real names. One—from someone who was *really* worried about staying anonymous—was made out of cutout magazine letters. The funny thing about that one was that all the writer was looking for was "a loving soul to share cooking classes and cello duets."

"Where do you *find* these people?" Nancy asked after a couple of minutes.

Lena laughed. "Oh, they find us, and more come in each week. Any clues so far?"

"No, I don't see anything that sounds like it could be the guy I'm looking for."

Nancy put the stack of ads down on Lena's desk. As she did so, that morning's edition of the *Record* caught her eye. "Could I take a look at this?" she asked. "I didn't have a chance when I left the house this morning."

"Be my guest."

Nancy skimmed the news, then picked up the section with the Personals in it. "These are the same as yesterday's, aren't they?" she asked.

"Oh, yes," said Lena. "We only update them once a week."

Nancy had already read that column the day before. She was about to turn past that page when something suddenly caught her eye. It was the last ad on the page.

"N.D.," it began, "I warned you last night. You'd better listen to me. Keep out of my way, or you'll be sorry."

Chapter

Eight

"Lena, LOOK AT this!" Nancy's eyes were bright as she pushed the paper toward the other woman. "How do you think it could have gotten in?"

"I—I have no idea," Lena said slowly. She looked amazed. "The ads run for an entire week, and we only update them once a week. We're not due to add new ones for another couple of days. And I see all the new ads before they go in! However this was done, it wasn't through the normal channels."

Obviously not, Nancy thought, at least not if Lena was the "normal channels." She read the ad again.

"'I warned you last night,'" she said out loud. "That can only be the guy who called me when I got home. Sure works fast, whoever he is."

"It sounds like you're in real danger," Lena said. She sounded more nervous than Nancy.

"Yes, but that's just the way it goes," Nancy said. "I'm *not* planning to stay out of his way, if that's what you mean."

"Working hard, or hardly working?" came a bright voice in back of her. Nancy turned to see Lucy Price, the girl she'd met the day before, standing next to the cubicle. "Come on, girls!" she continued. "Stop gabbing."

Nancy and Lena glanced quickly at each other, and Nancy gave a barely perceptible shake of her head. There was no point in telling Lucy anything, no matter how nice she seemed. Until Nancy had a better idea of who she was dealing with, she'd have to keep as quiet as possible.

"What's the matter? Can't we take a break once in a while?" she asked easily.

"Yeah. What are you—a slave driver?" Lena chimed in. It was a pretty lame comeback, Nancy thought, but at least Lena sounded as if she were trying to be more friendly. Nancy gave her an approving smile and noticed with satisfaction that Lucy Price looked surprised that Lena was responding with something other than a sulky look.

"Well, don't let *me* disturb your party," Lucy said cheerfully. "I just came over to see if you

57

have any paper clips. I'm not leaving the office today until my desk is completely organized."

"I don't," Lena answered. "And as a matter of fact, I'm out of a lot of supplies. I was just about to go to the mailroom and get some."

"I'll do it," Nancy offered. It would give her a chance to do some investigating on her own. "What do you need?"

Both women gave her a short list of the supplies they wanted. "I'm glad you're doing this, not me," Lucy said. "I go down there so many times that they think I'm hoarding the stuff. Don't tell them any of it's for me, okay?"

"Sure," said Nancy with a smile. "Just don't ever make me get extra desserts for you in a buffet line. My friend Bess does that already."

She headed down to the mailroom. Its vestibule was piled high with unopened packages, review copies of books, and office supplies. As she threaded her way gingerly through this obstacle course, Nancy suddenly heard a thud—and a yelp of pain—coming from inside the mailroom.

"I'm dying!" yelled a man's voice.

Nancy rushed inside the room. It was even more cluttered than the vestibule, if that was possible. In one corner, a thin young man was doubled up on the floor clutching his foot and moaning. Two of his coworkers were looking down at him calmly and making no move at all to help him.

"What's the matter?" she asked, walking right

up to the three men. "Can I do something? Are you hurt?" she asked the man on the floor.

"Oh, Bill's okay," said one of the men watching him. He grinned at her, his freckled face so good-natured that Nancy couldn't help smiling back. "Mr. Walking Wounded just dropped a stapler on his foot, that's all. We go through this kind of thing all the time."

"Come on, guys! It's killing me!" groaned Bill. "I don't think I'm going to be able to walk on it."

"Yeah, yeah." The second man sighed. "You'd better just forget about him. He always takes a long time to recover from these major injuries.

"Now, can I do something for *you?*" he asked. "I'm Todd Hill, by the way, and the carrot head is Steve Rudman—and the invalid writhing at your feet is Bill Stark."

"My name's Nancy Drew. I just need some supplies for the woman I'm working with—but are you sure you're okay, Bill?" she broke off to say.

He smiled weakly up at her and climbed a little shamefacedly to his feet. "I'm really not faking it," he said, shaking her hand. He had the lightest blue eyes she'd ever seen. "It's just that I'm sensitive to pain. I guess I'll live, though."

"Probably so, worse luck," said Todd.

Bill ignored him. "Anyway, thanks," he said to Nancy. "Now, you said you needed some supplies?"

"*I'll* get them. *I'll* get them," said Todd. "You'd

better just sit down and take it easy, Bill. It's not every day such a pretty girl walks in here—might give you some kind of relapse. What do you need, Nancy?"

Nancy handed him the list, and he headed over to the supply closet. "You say you're bringing this to someone you're working for?" he called back to her.

"Yes," Nancy said. "Lena Verle. I'm helping her for a few days."

"Helping that crab?" Steve Rudman asked. "What could you possibly do to help *her?*"

Nancy was glad she had rehearsed an answer just in case someone asked her that very question. "I'm kind of a temp," she said. "There's been such an increase in the mail the paper's getting that Mr. Whittaker thought she could use a part-time assistant. I'll probably just be here a few days, until things are a little more in control."

"Well, you can replace her anytime, as far as I'm concerned," said Steve. "I couldn't think of a worse person to handle the Personals."

"Actually, Lena's pretty nice," Nancy said casually. "But why do you say that?"

Steve snorted. "Writing one of those ads is an art. Why should someone have to hand it over to a woman who has no idea what a personal life even is? I bet she never goes home. She probably lives here."

"So you read the Personals?" Nancy asked quickly.

"Of course he does," Todd said, staggering out of the supply closet with his arms full of boxes. "One of these days, he's going to meet the ideal woman. So's Bill. So am I, for that matter. We're taking bets on who'll be first—unless *you're* the ideal woman. Are you?"

"Obviously," Nancy said brightly.

Todd clapped her on the back, dropping a whole box of pens onto the floor. "Way to go!" he crowed. "Well, which one of us lucky bachelors wins the dream date?"

This was getting a little out of hand. "Sorry, guys, I'm already taken," Nancy said. She had to force herself to put Ned out of her mind as she spoke. It was impossible to keep bantering with them when just the thought of him made her want to rush to the hospital to be with him.

"Could you tell me a little bit about what you all do here?" she asked. She didn't think it would have any bearing on the case, but she'd learned to collect information—no matter what kind —whenever she had the chance. She could never tell when it would be useful.

Bill Stark laughed. "We just about run the paper, that's all. Giving out supplies is the least of it. We're really kind of like a little private post office down here. We deliver all the incoming mail to the staff and send out all the outgoing. We send telexes and telegrams and okay all the overnight deliveries—and you wouldn't believe how often these people say something *has* to get there overnight. Also, we have the best coffee machine." He gestured toward a scarred old percolator on the counter.

"You say you deliver the incoming mail?" Nancy said. "Do you open it first?"

All three men looked slightly surprised. "Well, yes," Todd said at last. "We're supposed to. It's not as if we're trying to snoop around or anything."

"Oh, I didn't mean to suggest that," Nancy hastened to assure him. "I was just wondering if you read the Personals ads before you take them to Lena."

"No, no! Anything for her is supposed to be delivered unopened," said Bill. "Mr. Whittaker wants to keep the Personals as confidential as possible."

"What about the people who send in the ads to her? Do you ever see any of them?" Nancy asked.

"Wait a minute," Steve put in. "Why don't you just ask Lena Verle? What are you trying to get out of us, Nancy?"

"Nothing!" Nancy said. "It's just that I'm new on the job, and—" Suddenly she decided to level with them—at least partway. There couldn't be any harm in telling them about the mysterious ad aimed at her.

"I shouldn't tell you guys this, but maybe you can help me," she said, choosing her words carefully. "I've only been here for two days, and it's starting to look as though someone has it in for me. Have any of you read today's paper yet?"

All three of them shook their heads.

"Well, there's an ad that I think's written to me, and—wait, I'll get a copy." She dashed out of the mailroom and back to her desk.

"Hey! Where's my stuff?" Lucy Price yelled.

"I'll be right back," Nancy called back over her shoulder, running out.

"Here," she said breathlessly when she rejoined the three men. "Look at this. I was just wondering if any of you might have seen the person who dropped off this letter. That's all."

All three men bent their heads over the paper. "Wow, this guy sounds like a real sicko," Todd said after a minute. "Why's he bothering you, anyway?"

"I—I'm not really sure," Nancy said, lying. "Maybe it's someone who doesn't want me working here or something."

Bill was looking puzzled. "But you say you're just a temp?"

"Well, yes, kind of," said Nancy, wishing her rehearsed story had explained things better.

"Well, then, why would someone want you out of here?" he asked. "The only person who could get an ad in in the middle of the week like this would be someone who worked for the paper. But if you're just working here as a temp, why would anyone want you off the job?"

"Wait a minute," Nancy said. "Why does it have to be someone who works for the paper?"

"Well," said Bill, "the Personals column is only updated once a week. The new ads always come out in the Sunday paper. Only someone who knows how to get a new ad into the computer can have them printed—all our typesetting is computerized. Now here's a brand-new ad out on Tuesday. How could it have come from outside?"

"He's right," Todd put in. "Whoever it was would have had to slip the ad past Lena Verle to get it printed now."

Nancy's lips were a tight line. She could think of one person who'd wanted her out of this job even though she was just a "temp." She could think of one person who'd have no trouble slipping an extra ad into the paper. Lena Verle.

"So Lena *is* out to get me!" she said under her breath.

Chapter

Nine

LISTEN, GUYS, I have to get back to work,"
Nancy said abruptly. She wanted to get through
the confrontation with Lena as quickly as possible. "It's been nice talking to you, though.
Thanks a lot."

"Hey! Aren't you going to take your supplies?"
Todd called after her.

"Oh! Yes, of course. Thanks." Nancy turned
around and scooped the boxes into her arms. She
had forgotten about the original reason she had
come down there.

"Well, it's been real," Steve said as Nancy
whirled around to leave for the second time.

Back at Lena's cubicle, Nancy dumped the

supplies unceremoniously on the desk. "Here you go," she snapped before a surprised Lena had had time to say anything. "So. You still have it in for me, is that it?"

Lena looked honestly bewildered. "In for you?" she echoed.

"The guys in the mailroom just told me that only someone from the paper could have placed that ad. And there's only one person on this paper—as I figure—who wants me out of here. You."

"But I *don't* want you out of here anymore," Lena protested. "Haven't we been through this already? I had nothing to do with that ad!"

"You're the only person who could—" Nancy stopped short. She had just caught sight of a piece of stationery on Lena's desk. The reason she noticed it was that it had Lena's initials on it. And some kind of message—a message that didn't look friendly.

Nancy reached over and picked up the piece of paper. "Hey!" Lena protested, but Nancy was already reading aloud. " 'Dear Lena: Enclosed is a message for next week's Personals column. Thanks for bending the deadline this once.' " Nancy glanced quickly at Lena, who looked stunned. " 'And the message,' " she continued, " 'in case you've forgotten, is this: Watch out, N.D. If you don't get out of here, expect the worst. You'll get it.' Well, Lena? Who sent you this?"

"I—I've never seen it before!" Lena stammered.

"That's funny. Whoever wrote it seems to know *you* awfully well." Nancy sat down in the chair next to Lena's desk and rubbed her eyes wearily. "Come on, Lena," she said. "You'd make it a lot easier for yourself if you'd just tell me who wrote the letter. I'm going to find out, anyway, and it'll save us both time."

Lena opened her mouth, then shut it again. "I swear I don't know who sent that. You can believe me or not. It's up to you. But I can't tell you who sent that letter, because I don't know."

Nancy was silent for a second. "What can I say? I don't believe you. I can't force you to tell me anything, so I guess there's no point in going on with this right now. You don't mind if I hang on to the note, do you?" She was standing and putting the piece of paper into her purse as she spoke.

"Where—where are you going?" But Nancy didn't answer.

She was going upstairs to talk to Mr. Whittaker. Not to tattle on Lena. Nancy wasn't about to make any accusations unless she had definite proof. But at the moment, Mr. Whittaker seemed to be her only ally.

"No, I have to admit I hadn't noticed this ad," Mr. Whittaker told her a few minutes later, shaking his head with disbelief. "But the men in the mailroom are right. Only someone on the staff could have inserted this. And that can only mean that—it's hard to believe, but—"

"That whoever placed today's ad also placed the original one, the one Bess answered?" Nancy finished for him. "It's the only explanation I can think of, too. There's no reason anyone on the staff should want me off this case otherwise."

That meant that the "accident" with the bricks on the scaffolding probably hadn't been a coincidence at all.

"Well, do you have any suspects?"

"As a matter of fact, I do, but—" Nancy stopped short. She had just realized something. Mr. Whittaker might be a suspect himself.

But how can he be? she thought. The editor in chief of the *Record?* It was impossible to imagine him being involved.

On the other hand—now that she thought about it—he did fit Bess's description of the guy she had met in the restaurant. And Nancy had known plenty of criminals who seemed incapable of doing anything wrong. As far as opportunity went, Mr. Whittaker was as much a suspect as anyone else.

"Nancy? Are you there?" he asked her, smiling. "I said, do you have any suspects?"

Nancy forced herself to smile back. "Of course I do. But I know you'll understand that I should keep them to myself for now."

"I understand."

"There's one thing I'd like to do, though," Nancy said, "and that's to get Bess over here to look around. If she recognizes anyone, the case'll be over today."

"Well, I—I suppose that would be all right." Was it her imagination, or did he suddenly look wary?

"Great!" Nancy said enthusiastically. "I'll call her right away. Do you think I could make the call from your office? I'd rather not broadcast this any further than I have to."

"Absolutely," said Mr. Whittaker. "I'll let you have a little privacy, too." Before Nancy could tell him that it wasn't really necessary, he had left the room.

He really does seem nice, Nancy thought as she dialed Bess's number. *I'd hate to think he could be involved in this.*

She sighed in frustration when she got a busy signal. Wasn't any part of the case going to go her way?

Five minutes and three calls later, the line was still busy. *I'll just try once more,* Nancy thought —and on the last try she got Bess.

"Nancy! I heard about Ned. How is he?" Bess asked as soon as she heard Nancy's voice.

"He's doing okay. It's a long story. But that's not why I called." Quickly Nancy filled Bess in on everything that had happened. "Could you come down here and take a look around?" she finished.

"Sure I'll come over," her friend said, "if I *have* to. Is it okay if I bring George with me?"

"Sure," Nancy said.

"All right. See you in half an hour."

"Bess!" Nancy said in the split second before Bess hung up. "What was the name of that guy's friend—the one he said you'd murdered?"

"The Glove, he said. Why?"

"I'm just going to see if I can turn up anything about him in the morgue."

"The morgue!" Bess shrieked. "You're going to the morgue?"

Nancy smiled. "The *newspaper* morgue. The reference files here. Whoever the Glove was, he may have made the papers when he was murdered."

"Nan, I'm going to hang up before you tell me something that will make me even more nervous."

Bess would have been a *lot* more nervous if she'd been reading over Nancy's shoulder a few minutes later. The *Record*'s library had the past ten years of newspapers on microfiche. It didn't take Nancy long to discover that the Glove's death *had* made the papers. And it was a pretty gruesome death.

The man's real name wasn't the Glove, of course. It was John Engas, and he was an ex-con who had done time for armed robbery and forgery. He'd been in violation of his parole to be in Chicago at all, and the police had apparently never discovered what he was doing there. He had been killed in a traffic accident that had left his body so mangled that it took days to identify the remains. Yes, Nancy thought, it was a good thing Bess wasn't there reading right then.

Whoever the guy placing the ads was, his having been friends with John Engas didn't say much for him. But why had he accused Bess of leaving the Glove to die? Engas's body had been the only one in the car, and there was no evidence that he'd had any passengers.

Nancy rubbed her eyes. Boy, she thought, you could go blind reading off these machines. She was just about to turn off the microfiche machine when another article caught her eye.

"STILL NO SUSPECTS IN FIRST LINCOLN ROBBERY," said the headline. One of Chicago's biggest banks had been robbed in broad daylight, and the robbers were still at large. None of the money stolen had made its way back into circulation. In fact, the police had found no clues at all.

Something about the robbery sounded familiar, though. Was it the date? Quickly Nancy checked the story about John Engas again. Yes, the robbery and his car accident had taken place on the same day.

Was it possible that there was a connection between the two events? Engas had been previously jailed for robbery. He had violated his parole to be in Chicago at the time of the robbery. Maybe he had robbed First Lincoln himself!

No cash had been found in the car, Nancy reminded herself. Still, it was an awfully strange coincidence—if it was a coincidence.

Nancy checked her watch. She'd have to think about all this later. Bess and George would be there any minute now.

She decided to go up to walk past Mr. Whittaker's office before going down to her floor. "Your friend on the way?" he asked.

"She'll be here any minute," Nancy said cheerfully. And you're the first person I'll introduce her to, she thought.

"Oops! Sorry, Bill," she said. She had just collided with Bill Stark as she was turning away from Mr. Whittaker's office.

"Did I hear you say someone's coming to visit?" he asked.

"My friend Bess Marvin," Nancy answered. "I'm just giving her a look around the place."

"Well, bring her down to the mailroom!" Bill urged.

Nancy smiled. "You bet I will," she said.

She was relieved to see that Lena wasn't sitting at her desk when she got there. But the phone was ringing steadily.

"Lena left early. She said she wasn't feeling well. Now, pick up that phone!" Lucy Price called over to her. "It's been ringing for *hours!*"

Nancy looked at her watch again. Bess and George were probably waiting for her downstairs —but she had to answer this anyway. She picked up the receiver. "Personals," she said.

"I—I'd like to answer one of your ads," said a girl's voice at the other end. "Is this the right place for that?"

"Well, the regular editor's away from her desk now," said Nancy, "and we don't usually take ads over the phone. But why don't you leave your message? If the editor needs more information, she can get in touch with you."

"Okay," said the girl. "Here it is. 'Sorry it took you so long to catch up with me. I'll meet you on Tuesday at eight o'clock at the coffee shop on Fortieth and East. Signed, the Blonde in White.'"

Nancy's heart was racing, but she forced herself to speak calmly. "Fortieth—and—East," she repeated, writing it down.

But that was that very night! "Miss, I'm afraid—" Nancy began. But the person at the other end had already hung up.

There was no way the ad could get in that day's paper. It was already out. And whoever had been calling seemed to have forgotten that she'd have to pay for the ad before it could run at all.

But it was just the clue Nancy had been looking for. Nancy could hardly believe her good luck. The mystery man won't read this in time, so I won't be able to catch him with this girl, she thought. But if *I* can meet her, she may turn out to be the key to the whole mystery!

"Where's your friend?"

Nancy jumped, startled out of her thoughts. Bill was standing beside her desk.

"Bill! Hi," Nancy said. "I'm just going down to the lobby to meet her now."

But she never got there. When the elevator door slid open, Nancy was almost knocked down by a woman who careened blindly toward her. It was Dawn, the receptionist from downstairs —but there was something terribly wrong with her.

Dawn's eyes were wide with terror, and her face was white. She veered crazily into the middle of the newsroom.

"Someone just called and said there's a bomb in the building! It's set to go off any second!" she shrieked.

Chapter
Ten

FOR AN INSTANT the newsroom was completely silent. Then one person screamed—and everyone leaped from his seat and moved to the elevators where Nancy was standing.

"Move!" one reporter snarled at her as he reached past her to push the elevator button. "The stupid thing is stuck!" he said, pounding on the button. Behind him, people were trying to move forward.

Nancy tried to stand where she was, but the force of the crowd was sucking her along. She knew that if things didn't calm down, someone would be hurt—long before any bomb could go off. Elbowing her way to one side of the room, she scrambled onto a desk and whistled piercingly.

There was a momentary lull as people turned to look at her. Nancy didn't waste any time.

"We've got to calm down or no one will make it out of here in one piece!" she shouted. To her relief, she saw that everyone was focused on her and listening. "Now," she said, "the stairs are safer than the elevators in case a fire should break out. We need to form lines and go down that way. *Carefully.*"

"She's right." It was Mr. Whittaker, pushing his way to the front of the crowd. "I just called security, and they're asking everyone to evacuate the building by the stairs. The police are on their way over. Now, if you'll all just file out in an orderly manner, there shouldn't be any problems."

He propped open the door leading to the stairway. "Good," he said after listening a minute. "The other floors are already on their way down. Let's start down now," Mr. Whittaker said, and gave Nancy a gentle shove on the shoulder.

Out on the landing, she glanced nervously around her. She hadn't realized so many people worked in the building. What seemed like an endless parade was snaking its way down —agonizingly slowly.

In the dim light, the procession on the stairs had a ghostly quality. No one was saying much.

"The mayor's press secretary is supposed to be calling me right now," one woman remarked in a doleful voice as she checked her watch. "I hope they're not mad."

Nancy turned her mind from the scene and thought about her two friends. Had Bess and George arrived by now? Were they in the building somewhere—maybe even taking the elevator up to Nancy's floor? Or had someone managed to keep them from going inside? Nancy knew Bess would be worried about her.

Nancy was also wondering if the bomb threat was just another "coincidence." The timing seemed so convenient. Just after she had finally managed to reach Bess, Dawn had gotten the phone call warning her about the bomb. Could it be that someone had called Dawn just to make sure Bess couldn't come and check out the staff?

At least that meant there probably *wasn't* a bomb in the building, Nancy thought. Then a harsh, clanging bell jangled loudly just above her head.

"It's the bomb! It's about to go off!" screamed a man's voice on the flight of stairs above—and Bill Stark came hurtling down the stairs.

"Let me out of here!" he moaned, trying to force his way to the front of the line. "We're all going to die!"

Abruptly the bell stopped ringing, but Bill didn't stop panicking. He was struggling so fiercely to get down that he knocked one woman over. "I've got to get out of this place!" he moaned again.

"Stop that, Bill!" Nancy ordered as he came abreast of her. She grabbed him by the shoulders and forced him to look at her. The others stared at this small drama, shaking their heads as they continued to file down the steps.

Bill was struggling against her hands. "It's no good," he whimpered. "We'll die like rats in here! We'll be buried alive—"

Nancy gritted her teeth. She gripped his shoulder even more tightly, so he couldn't get away. "It's probably just a threat, not a real bomb," she said. "You're just making it harder on everyone."

"Sorry," he muttered after a minute.

"It's okay," Nancy said in a friendlier voice. "Can you make it down okay now?"

"I—I think so. Thanks, Nancy." He seemed embarrassed. Head down, he slipped back into line without saying anything more.

There were four flights to walk down from the newsroom, and then they were outside. Walking into the fresh, misty air felt like stepping out of prison. Nancy turned her face gratefully toward the sky to meet the light rain, and smiled. They'd made it!

"Nancy, there you are!" came Bess's voice at her elbow. George was right behind her cousin. "We were worried sick about you! When we got here, the security guards wouldn't let us in, and they wouldn't tell us why, either. We kept badgering them and badgering them until one of them finally told us what was going on. Then we were sorry we'd asked. Are you sure you're okay?"

"I don't *think* I've blown up yet," Nancy assured her, smiling. "But listen, Bess. This bomb scare may actually be a blessing in disguise. With everyone on the staff outside here, it'll be easier to see if you recognize anyone. Let's sort of stroll around."

Casually the three girls began walking through the different clusters of *Record* staffers.

Now that people felt safer, the atmosphere had turned festive despite the light rain. People stood around in little groups, laughing and talking as though they were at a party. "This is like being let out of school early!" Nancy heard a woman say as she walked by. "You're right," another woman answered. *"Now* I wouldn't mind seeing the place blow up."

The arrival of a bomb squad, two wailing police cars, and a fire engine only seemed to heighten the excitement. "Stand back, please. Stand back, please," the police kept saying patiently as they tried to push their way through the crowds that were trying eagerly to see what was going on.

When several dark-suited figures had disappeared into the building—with two German shepherds panting and straining at their leashes

—an expectant silence fell over the crowd. In a few minutes a man with a megaphone came out to the front door.

"The building will be closed for the rest of the day," he announced. "Mr. Whittaker has asked me to tell you that all nonessential personnel are free to go home. The printing of the paper will take place at our annex across the street."

There was a murmur from the crowd. "Hmmm. I wonder if *I'm* essential," joked Lucy Price, who was standing near Nancy. "I don't think I'll wait around to find out."

Already the crowd was thinning out. Nancy turned to Bess. "Any luck?" she asked.

"Not yet. I keep thinking I recognize people and then realize it's because I saw them here yesterday. I might as well keep trying until everyone's left, though."

The crowd had thinned out so fast that almost everyone was gone. "I'm sorry, Nan," Bess said at last. "I just don't see Mr. Wrong."

Nancy sighed. "That would have made things too easy, I guess. Thanks for trying, though."

"How's Ned doing?" George asked.

"Oh—" Nancy poured out her story once again. "I'm just so happy he's regained consciousness. He looks pretty bad, and the doctor's not sure whether he'll be able to play sports this fall. But I'm sure the worst is behind him. I wish I felt as optimistic about the case."

"I'm sure you'll get a break soon," Bess said

comfortingly. "I just wish I had never answered that dumb ad. If it hadn't been for me, none of this would have happened.

"On the other hand," Bess said more cheerfully, "if I hadn't answered the ad, some sicko would still be out there scaring people—only he wouldn't have Nancy Drew on his trail. Someday, when you've caught him, River Heights will thank me for having been so stupid."

Nancy had to laugh at that.

"Bess said you were going to look through the files in the morgue," said George. "Did anything turn up?"

"I'm not sure. Maybe. But—I almost forgot in all this excitement—I got the most incredible phone call just before we came down! Bess, I think I may have heard from the girl *you* were supposed to be."

"You'd better be careful," Bess said soberly when Nancy had described the strange message she'd received upstairs. "What if this girl *did* somehow cause the Glove's death?"

"That's what I hope I'll find out," said Nancy. "I'm going to meet her tonight."

"Want some company?" George asked. "You'd better say yes because this could be dangerous. It just doesn't make sense for you to go alone."

"Okay," Nancy said. "Well, I've got the rest of the day off—and I guess I can't give you a tour of the place. So let's go get something to eat."

* * *

"Uh, Nan?" said George later that night. "I don't *see* a coffee shop on Fortieth and East. Are you sure that's what that girl said?" George slowed down and pulled over to the curb.

"Absolutely. I wrote it down while she was talking." Nancy peered out of George's windshield. It was true. There wasn't a coffee shop in sight. "She must have made a mistake! My first real break in this case, and it gets messed up like this!"

"Should we head back home?" asked Bess hopefully.

"No. Absolutely not," replied Nancy. "I'm going to wait here. She may still show up."

"Unless she gave you the wrong address, and now she's waiting at a coffee shop somewhere else," George pointed out.

"Oh, no. You may be right." Nancy paused for a minute. "Well, look," she said, undoing her seat belt. "I'll wait here for half an hour. You guys drive around and see if you can find a coffee shop on any other corner around here. If you do—and *especially* if you see a blond girl dressed in white at one of them—come right back and get me."

It's a little hard to believe there's a coffee shop anywhere around here, she thought as she positioned herself in the middle of the sidewalk. Fortieth and East was squarely in the middle of the warehouse district. There was nothing around but empty, dark buildings and cars parked like silent spectators in rows along the curb.

It was dark now. And Nancy was starting to feel conspicuous standing alone in the middle of a sidewalk at night. But after ten minutes she heard the welcome sound of a car driving toward her. She squinted toward its headlights. Then she heard footsteps behind her.

Before Nancy could turn, something smashed into the back of her head.

The blow knocked her out instantly. She didn't even feel it as someone dragged her to the edge of the road and draped her, facedown, over the curb.

Chapter
Eleven

BESS, I'M *OKAY*," Nancy protested for the fifth time. "I had a good night's sleep. I had breakfast and lunch in bed. The swelling's down. I feel great!"

"I still think you're crazy," said Bess. "Why don't you just spend the rest of the day in bed?"

It was Wednesday afternoon, the day after Bess and George had found Nancy in the street, and they were checking to see how she was doing. Although her face was still bruised, and the back of her head felt tender, Nancy had decided it was time to get out of bed. When her friends got to her house, she had just finished taking a shower.

When Bess and George hadn't found a coffee

shop in the near vicinity the night before, they had come back to see how Nancy was doing. When they'd reached her corner, she was just starting to struggle to her feet.

Of course there'd been no sign of her assailant. There was no way of knowing whether it had been the girl in white or someone else. Nancy had insisted that she was well enough to go home. *"I* don't have a concussion," she'd said, and after a horrified Hannah had checked Nancy's eyes to verify she didn't have a concussion, Nancy collapsed into bed. Now all she wanted to do was get back on the job.

"If I spend any more time 'recovering,' I'll lose my mind," she told her friends. "I just want to head back to the paper for a couple of hours. I want to go through the files again, and the morgue closes at six."

"We'd better let her do it," George told Bess. "She has that look in her eyes. Just call us when you get back, Nan."

"You know what you *could* do for me, though," Nancy said, "is to stop in and see how Ned's doing. I'd do it myself, but I don't want him to see me all bruised like this. The doctor doesn't want me reminding him of the case."

"Where do you want us to say you are?" asked George.

"Tell him—tell him—oh, just tell him I've been delayed. Tell him I promise I'll call him tonight. And give him my love."

"Sure," said George with a grin. "We'll take him some kind of potted plant, too. A nice spidery potted plant is just the thing for an invalid."

Nancy laughed. "I can see you'll do a better job of cheering him up today than I possibly could."

A light rain was falling as Nancy emerged from the lobby of the *Record* building a couple of hours later. Her second search through the paper's files had made her more suspicious than ever that "the Glove," John Engas, had robbed First Lincoln in Chicago.

"How could you leave the Glove to die?" the man in the restaurant had asked Bess. Obviously he thought the girl he was looking for was some kind of suspect in Engas's death. And a robber, too? Nancy wondered. If she'd somehow killed Engas and made off with the haul from the bank . . . But how could she have organized a car accident like the one that had killed him?

Nancy was still puzzling it over as she got into her Mustang and headed for home. But as she pulled out of the parking lot, she noticed a car speeding away from the building in the opposite direction from the way she was going.

A dark blue sedan with a dented front fender.

That's the car that hit Ned! Nancy thought. I've got to catch it!

With a squeal of brakes she turned the Mustang around and took off after the sedan. For about five seconds she thought she had a good chance of catching up to it. Then she reached the main road.

"I don't believe this," Nancy muttered. It was four-thirty. What with the beginning of rush hour and the rain—which was now falling more heavily—traffic was unbearably snarled. She could just see the dark blue sedan two blocks ahead of her. It was moving as slowly as her Mustang—but if it managed to break free of this jam before she did, she'd never catch up.

A red light. Nancy tapped the steering wheel in frustration. In the car next to hers, a man was happily bopping his head back and forth to the beat of his radio, oblivious to the mess of cars around him. He caught her eye and winked, still twitching to the music. Nancy looked away.

Green light. The Mustang inched forward through the intersection, its wipers swishing monotonously back and forth. Past a group of girls laughing on the sidewalk, a baby being pushed along in a stroller with an umbrella over it, a dog sniffing idly at the curb. Taking advantage of the stalled traffic, an old woman threaded her way across the street between the cars. She gave Nancy a pleasant wave as she passed in front of the Mustang. Nancy waved back, but she was feeling too edgy to smile.

Was the dark blue sedan pulling out of traffic up there? It was! It had managed to break free of the pack and was turning left onto Sycamore Street. Nancy was still trapped behind two intersections—and there was another red light ahead of her. But she couldn't let the other car get away!

Nancy thought quickly. Sycamore Street, she knew, led to Monroe Avenue, which in turn led to the expressway. It was safe to assume the other driver was heading that way—he'd be too easy to catch if he stayed in street traffic. If Nancy could make a left turn herself at the next intersection, she could get onto Monroe and—just possibly —catch up with him. But how?

She glanced quickly into the oncoming lane, switched on her emergency flashers, and leaned hard on the horn. Then she pulled out of her own lane and started driving down the middle of the street.

"Get off the road, idiot!" a burly man in the car ahead of her yelled furiously. Cars on both sides of her were honking and swerving to get out of her way. Nancy's palms were damp on the steering wheel, but she stared resolutely at the yellow divider. Traffic was moving so slowly that none of the cars around her was in any danger, and she *had* to make that turn. Just a few more feet, and she'd reach the intersection.

There she was—and fortunately, the light was still red. Holding her breath, Nancy inched out into the intersection. One car from the left passed in front of her, then another—and then there was a space. She floored the accelerator and whipped the steering wheel to the left, cutting just in front of a truck. Its horn blasted angrily, but Nancy didn't care. The road ahead of her was clear. She still had a chance to catch the blue sedan!

In a second she had reached Monroe. She turned right—and breathed a sigh of relief. She could see the car just one block ahead. And it was stopped at a red light.

Monroe Avenue had four lanes. Nancy cut into the left lane and drove as fast as she could. "Thank you," she murmured under her breath as the light turned green. She sped across the intersection into the same block as the sedan.

All she had to do was shift lanes twice, and she was just two cars behind the dark blue one. It went so smoothly that Nancy was sure the other driver hadn't even spotted her car. Maybe she was about to get lucky.

Nancy nosed the Mustang forward until it was almost tailgating the car ahead of her. When the light changed, she followed as closely as she dared. There was just one more light before they reached the entrance ramp to the expressway, and she was determined not to lose her quarry again. But would the sedan take the ramp going east, or the one going west?

The driver didn't signal. Maybe he *had* spotted her after all. He just made an abrupt left, narrowly missing an oncoming van, and darted onto the ramp heading east. With a sickening squeal of brakes the van swerved out of the way—and Nancy swooped onto the ramp in front of it, following the blue car.

Now I've got you, she thought, beginning to accelerate as she prepared to enter the expressway. Then she saw the orange sign.

ROAD LEGALLY CLOSED
PROCEED AT OWN RISK
STATE LIABILITY LIMITED

No wonder there were only the two of them on the ramp. Well, at least that meant there wouldn't be as many other drivers to worry about. And chasing a car—any car—on the open road would be nothing compared to what she had just gone through.

No, that wasn't true.

Just as it was about to reach the expressway, the dark blue car made a U-turn and screeched back down the one-way ramp. It was heading straight toward her. Then it was passing her on its way back down the ramp. Things had happened so fast that Nancy hadn't even gotten a glimpse of the driver.

But meanwhile she hadn't slowed down at all, and in another second, she'd be on the expressway! Should she make a U-turn, too?

No. As desperate as she was to catch him, Nancy knew she couldn't risk it. The danger of causing an accident was just too great. Instead, she'd pull over on the shoulder, get out of her car, and try to chase this creep on foot. She switched on her left blinker and pulled smoothly onto the expressway.

And then she heard it—a massive crash, behind her on the ramp. Nancy's stomach lurched. "Oh, no," she whispered.

The dark blue sedan must have hit something. The chase was over, and she didn't want to see the final outcome.

Suddenly Nancy felt as if she were in a speeded-up movie. She pulled over onto the shoulder of the expressway, grabbed her purse, and jumped out of the car. Should she lock her door? No, she'd need to get into the car quickly if she had to go for help. Her first-aid kit, though —she'd better get that—and the blanket. They were both in the trunk. Nancy yanked them out, slammed the trunk closed, and dashed back toward the entrance ramp.

What was left of the dark blue sedan was lying in a crumpled mass on its back about a hundred feet ahead of her. By some miracle there were no other cars on the ramp. The sedan must have hit the guard rail, ricocheted across the road, and flipped over.

Nancy was running as fast as she could toward the car, but her legs felt like lead. "Where is everyone?" she moaned to herself. "I know this road is closed, but it is *rush hour!*" If anyone could have survived that crash, how would she be able to help him all alone?

Now she was next to the wreck. Heart pounding, Nancy threw herself down on her hands and knees to peer inside the shattered window.

The car was empty.

Chapter

Twelve

NANCY STARED AT the empty car. Then she slowly rose to a standing position again and looked around her. "Where did he go?" she asked incredulously.

Had the driver somehow been thrown clear of the car? There was no sign of anyone on the road, and the car's windshield, though cracked, was still in place. Nancy bent down to look into the car again, just to be certain.

Then she noticed that the door by the driver's seat was slightly open. She leaned forward and gave it a gentle tug. From its upside-down position it opened as obediently as if the car had been brand-new.

"So he just opened the door and walked away," Nancy muttered. "It's as simple as that. Well, my friend, you're *still* not going to get away."

She jumped to her feet. The rain had started up again. A misty haze rose from the pavement and the strip of field bordering it. Beyond the field was the straggly edge of a forest whose trees loomed pale and ghostlike above a tangled mass of underbrush.

Nancy sighed. If the mysterious driver had somehow managed to hitch a ride, she'd never find him. She did decide to try looking for him in the woods before she went back to her car. She jotted down the wreck's license-plate number on a small pad in her purse and stepped gingerly into the cold, sodden grass. Instantly her heels sank into the mud. I *would* be wearing pumps, she thought.

By the time she had squelched her way across the strip of field, Nancy's shoes were clammy and her clothes were clinging to her in damp folds. The rain was coming down harder now, and it was getting dark. Nancy was glad there was a flashlight in the first-aid kit. She'd need it.

Now she was standing on drenched leaves at the edge of the woods, peering uncertainly into the trees. A rivulet of water trickled off a branch overhead and dripped right down her collar. Shivering, Nancy pulled out her flashlight and played the beam back and forth.

All it revealed were tree trunks, vines, and shadows. Well, what did you expect? Nancy asked herself. She pulled her blazer closer around her and stepped forward into the darkness.

A branch snapped in the dark ahead of her. Was it a footstep? As she struggled along through the heavy piles of fallen leaves, Nancy was suddenly sure someone was watching her.

Then a man stepped out from behind a tree into her path.

"Bill Stark!" Nancy exclaimed, surprised to see one of the mailroom employees from the *Record,* the one who had acted so scared during the bomb threat.

He laughed. "Nancy Drew!" he answered mockingly.

His pale eyes were glittering in the flashlight beam, and he was shivering uncontrollably. His hands were behind his back as if he were hiding something—a gun? He took another step toward her, but Nancy stood her ground.

Her mind was racing. How much did Bill know *she* knew? She had better try to sound as ignorant as she could—as though running into an acquaintance in the middle of the woods by an express ramp could happen to anyone.

"Is that *your* car back there?" she asked.

"You know it is," Bill answered.

"I—I can't believe it! You're so lucky to be alive! When I heard that car crash, I said to myself, 'Boy, whoever was in that car is in big trouble!'" Nancy knew she sounded inane, but maybe that would disarm him. "And *then,* when I saw that the car was *empty,* I started to wonder if I'd just been imagining things!" She forced a laugh and hoped it didn't sound as fake to Bill as it did to her.

But Bill didn't seem to be listening. "I told you to stay away," he growled.

"Oh, *you're* the one who left me that message? Well, that wasn't a very nice thing to do. Besides, you know how we girls are—tell us not to do a thing, and we just want to do it all the more!" Nancy was glad none of her friends was around to hear her.

"Yeah?" Bill said. "Well, that's too bad for you."

It wasn't working. Nancy decided to drop the ruse and try to gain his confidence. If he trusted her, he might be less likely to hurt her. She still couldn't tell if he had a gun, but it was wise to anticipate the worst.

"Okay, Bill," she said quietly. "I didn't mean to insult your intelligence. I just—I just got a little nervous." That was true, anyway. Being alone in the woods on a rainy night with a guy who had already tried to put her out of commission wasn't exactly soothing. "What's going on, anyway?" she continued. "Why do you have it in for me?"

"I told you to stay away!" Bill repeated. "Why couldn't you have left well enough alone? I wouldn't have hurt Bess—I just wanted to make sure she'd stay off my back!"

She had to try to keep him talking. "So you placed that first ad," she said.

"Of course I did. Your friend should never have butted in."

"Butted in? What are you talking about?"

Bill just continued as if he hadn't heard her. "She led me on. Making me think she was the right girl—and then I could tell she had no idea what I was talking about. Well, then, why'd she answer the ad in the first place?"

"So you weren't looking for a date," Nancy said, though she already knew the answer. "You needed to find the girl in white for another reason."

"Of course!" Bill said impatiently. "Do you think I'm the kind of guy who has to get a date through the Personals?"

His sudden show of pride was so unexpected that Nancy laughed. But she realized instantly that that had been a bad move. Bill's face went dark with rage.

"Then *you* had to butt in, too," he snarled, thrusting his face closer to hers. "I was watching when you brought her to the paper that first time. I have to give you credit—you still came into the building after I dumped those bricks."

"How'd you manage that, anyway?" Nancy asked in a tone of polite interest.

"Oh, I just happened to be up on the roof at

the time," Bill said offhandedly. "I've got a master key to the door up there. I recognized Bess and pushed the cart over the edge." He broke into a fit of coughing and stamped his feet to warm them. It was practically dark now, and the night was getting colder and colder. Nancy was shivering herself—whether from cold or tension she wasn't sure.

"I have to tell you, I couldn't believe it when I saw you two walk in," Bill went on. "And when I overheard your name—well, I know who the famous Nancy Drew is. I should have realized it would take more than a couple of phone calls to stop you."

"Yes," Nancy said bleakly. "Even hitting Ned didn't stop me." It was just starting to sink in that she was standing around talking to the guy who'd almost killed her boyfriend. It was hard to keep talking to him under the circumstances, but she had to get more of his story.

"Sorry about your boyfriend, by the way," Bill said. He sounded as if he was apologizing for spilling her coffee. "I meant to hit you, of course."

"Of course," Nancy echoed. "But don't be too hard on yourself. After all, you *did* manage to knock me out. If that was you last night, I mean."

"Yeah. I was standing and reading the message while you were writing it down. You didn't even know I was there. I decided to meet you there.

Too bad the girl in white didn't show up. You must have written the address down wrong."

Nancy ignored that. "And you're the one who made the bomb threat, too?" she asked.

"Well, what else could I do?" Bill complained. "I was keeping an eye on you—an ear, I should say." He laughed. "When I heard you tell Whittaker you were going to call Bess, I had to stop you somehow."

"I thought it was Lena," Nancy said, half to herself.

Bill snickered. "I knew you would. I put that fake message on her desk, too—the one asking her to run another ad midweek. Poor Lena. She never had a chance of getting you to believe her after that. Pretty smart, don't you think?"

"Brilliant," Nancy said sarcastically.

Bill didn't seem to notice her tone. "Flattery won't get you anywhere," he said darkly.

All right, Nancy thought. That's my cue.

She lowered the flashlight slightly, trying to see if there was any stick on the ground big enough to use as a weapon. "But you still haven't told me what that ad meant in the first place," she reminded Bill. "If you weren't advertising for a date, what *did* you want? And why did you keep asking Bess what she'd done with the money?" There was a broken-off branch about six feet to the left. Maybe she could edge toward it gradually.

"I've told you too much already," Bill snapped. "But I guess it doesn't matter. You won't get the chance to tell anyone else. What are you looking for?" he asked suddenly.

"Nothing. I—I just thought I'd dropped my car keys." Nancy was having trouble concentrating. Above the steady patter of the rain, she'd just noticed another sound: running water. There was a stream—or at least a brook—nearby, and Nancy thought it sounded as though it was in a gully of some kind. If she got desperate, she could run down the gully and try to escape that way. But she'd better leave that as a last resort.

"Well, Bill, I really have to hand it to you," she said. Maybe she could soothe him into a better mood. "You're one of the most intelligent guys I've ever tried to catch. How did you manage to—"

"Just shut up, will you?" snarled Bill. "I'm tired of talking to you. And anyway"—he was suddenly glaring suspiciously at her—"*I* didn't hear you drop any keys."

"Well, I can't find them in here. We may need them, Bill—you might want me to drive you somewhere." Nancy opened her purse and pretended to search it. The keys were lying right on top of her tissues, and she quickly closed her hand over them so they wouldn't jingle. "Oh, no! They're just not in here!" she moaned. "I know I heard them fall— Wait, are they there by your foot?"

Startled, Bill looked down—and in that split second Nancy grabbed the broken branch and jabbed him hard in the stomach. He doubled up and fell to the ground, and Nancy took off toward the rushing water she had heard.

He can't have a gun, she thought, or he'd have fired it by now. She ran even faster toward the watery sound.

Yes. It was a brook at the bottom of a steep twenty-foot slope. Without a second's pause Nancy scrambled down the slope. Wet branches kept slapping her in the face, and the spongy, leaf-covered hill was terrifyingly slippery underfoot, but she didn't let herself think about anything until she had reached the bottom.

Then she heard a crashing in the underbrush above. "I'll get you now, Drew!" Bill yelled furiously. He was coming after her.

Her flashlight! She'd forgotten all about it! Quickly Nancy switched it off. Then she began backing away, praying that the sound of the water would cover the sound of her footsteps.

"I can still see you," Bill called down in a terrifyingly calm voice. "You'll be better off if you just stop where you are. I'm not in the mood for another one of these chase scenes."

Maybe he was just bluffing. It was definitely too dark for Nancy to see *him*. She kept on backing away. One slow step backward, then another—

And then she tripped over a rock and reeled

over toward the brook, landing on her hands and knees in water so icy that she couldn't hold back a gasp.

"Oh, there you are!" Bill said in a happy little singsong. "Just hang on. I'll be right down to give you a hand."

Nancy heard the underbrush crackle as he stepped forward. "Hey!" he said sharply. "I can't—"

Suddenly he screamed, and Nancy heard him crashing down the slope. With a horrible thud he landed on the rocks below.

The only sound was the mocking gurgle of the brook.

Chapter

Thirteen

Nancy was still holding her flashlight. She switched it on and saw Bill Stark lying crumpled at the bottom of the gully. As she raced toward him, she had a horrible sense of déjà vu.

Only this time she wasn't racing toward her boyfriend but toward the man who had tried to kill her. And this time there was no one to help her. She was alone in the dark woods. Whatever happened to Bill would be entirely up to her.

She knelt down by Bill and gently touched his shoulder. His eyelids flickered and half opened. "No," he moaned. "What's—where am . . ." His eyes closed again, and he turned his head away.

So he was alive after all. I should leave you here, Nancy thought bitterly. Maybe that would give you time to think about what you did to Ned and Bess. But she knew she couldn't do that. She'd have to get help, and she'd have to figure out a way to take him with her.

First she had to get him to stay awake, though. She shook Bill's shoulder. "Bill? Bill, we have to get you out of here," she said urgently.

He moaned again. "Can't do it. It—hurts too much. Just let me sleep, okay?" And his head lolled sideways again. Nancy was sure he was in shock.

"I can't let you sleep. Can you tell me what hurts?"

"My leg. I think it's broken," Bill mumbled.

"Well, we can work around that. What about your arms? Can you move them?" She'd already seen him turn his head. If he could move his arms, too, she'd be reasonably sure his back wasn't injured.

"My arms are okay," Bill said. "It's just my leg. Why can't you go for help and let me rest here?" He didn't seem to notice that he was shivering.

"Because," Nancy said tightly, "you're soaked to the bone, for one thing. You'll keep warmer if you move—it may be a long time before we find someone to help. And because it might be a little hard for anyone to find you again in the dark." *And*, she thought to herself, because I'm not going to give you any possible chance to get away again.

"Look," she went on, "try to sit up. I'll pull your shoulders, and when I count to three, let's go for it."

"You're not strong enough," Bill said in a feeble voice.

"Oh, I think I can manage okay. Now. One —two—*three!*"

On "three" she pulled with all her strength. Bill was about as helpful as a bag of sand, but somehow Nancy finally positioned him in a wavering sit. Then she looked around until she found a stick he might be able to use as a crutch.

What a job, she thought. First I'm looking for sticks to hit him with, then to rescue him.

"That dirty piece of wood? It's all wet!" Bill whined when Nancy handed it to him.

Nancy's patience was starting to wear thin. "Look, just take the stick," she urged. "You may have forgotten the reason you're down here at all, but I haven't. I don't have to do this, you know. My perfectly good car's back up there waiting for me, and anytime you decide you'd like to get back up the hill on your own and drive yourself to the hospital in *your* car, just let me know."

There was a pause. "All right, help me stand up," Bill said at last.

Nancy pushed her sopping wet hair out of her eyes and sighed. It had taken her an hour to help

Bill out of the gully, and they still had the field to cross. "Want to take a break?" she asked, turning to Bill.

"Please," he gasped. In the beam of the flashlight his face looked ashen, and his eyes were rolling back in his head. He was obviously in a lot of pain and exhausted as well. If she hadn't suggested that they stop, Nancy suspected he might have fallen right where they were standing.

"Better not sit down again," she said in a kinder voice. "It might be too hard to get you back up. You can lean on my shoulder if that will help."

His hand on her shoulder was incredibly heavy. Nancy checked her watch. She'd give him five minutes, and then they'd struggle on. But when the five minutes were up, Nancy felt more tired than she had before they stopped.

"Look how close we are to the expressway now," she said encouragingly. "We'll be there in no time."

"I—I really can't go any farther," Bill said. "I'm not kidding, Nancy. You'd better just get back to your car and leave me here. I'll understand."

Nancy smiled wryly. "I think we're stuck with each other for the moment, Bill. Let's make the most of it."

"No. This is as far as I go."

"But we're almost there! You *can't* give up now," Nancy pleaded.

For answer Bill took his hand off her shoulder, spun around dizzily—and collapsed facedown on the ground. "No more nagging," Nancy heard him mutter into the grass.

Nancy forced herself to speak as cheerfully as possible. "Well, I'm sorry you feel that way," she said. "I guess I'm just going to have to drag you across the field." She waited for a second to see if that would galvanize him back up again, but he didn't move. "Okay. It's your decision." And she reached for his hands.

"Ooof!" she said, only half kidding. "What have they been feeding you?"

Bill didn't even bother to answer.

It was the longest walk Nancy had ever taken. Just trying to keep Bill's head from dragging along in the grass was as hard as pulling him. Her purse and first-aid kit kept slipping off her shoulder. To make matters even worse, the sticky mud underfoot finally wrenched the heel off one of her pumps. And—just to cheer things up—it began to pour again, this time with thunder and lightning mixed in.

Oh, my little heated car, Nancy thought longingly as she hobbled along. A warm bed and a dry bathrobe. *Food*—she hadn't had a thing since lunch. Why did I ever think I wanted an interesting job?

And she hadn't seen a single car pass since they'd gotten out of the woods. Maybe—on top of the road's being legally closed—there was a storm warning out. I can't drive in this rain, Nancy realized. I'll have to wait until it lets up.

There they were at last at the dark, shining express ramp. At least it would be easier to drag Bill over asphalt than grass. There was his wrecked car being tirelessly washed by rain. "The police can send a tow truck for it," she called down to him.

Now they were leaving the ramp, and there —at last—was her car. "We made it!" she shouted at Bill. "We're safe!"

Somehow she managed to run the last few feet to the car. Bill didn't seem heavy at all now. Nancy unlocked the car door and hoisted him into the passenger seat. Then she raced around to the other side and let herself in.

"Now. Ignition. And lights. And heat," she chattered, turning the heat on full blast. *"And* flashers. I'm sorry I don't have anything hot to drink, but there's plenty of water out there if you get thirsty."

"Why are you being so nice?" mumbled Bill, wincing as he shifted position in the seat.

"Just my job," said Nancy. "Now, keep an eye out for any headlights—on either side of the highway. We'll try to flag down help if anyone goes by. I'm going to stay in here and keep you company until I actually see a car coming. No sense in standing out there for hours. I'll just have my flashlight ready in case."

Bill didn't answer. He looked as if he'd dropped off to sleep already. After a couple of minutes Nancy switched the radio on low to keep herself company.

"Rain and gale winds to continue on through the night," said the announcer. "There's a travelers' advisory in effect until further notice. So stay inside and keep warm with someone you love."

I wish, thought Nancy as she turned the heat up a notch. Ned, I just hope you're more comfortable than I am.

Bill muttered something inaudible, and Nancy glanced over at him. He was looking worse and worse—flushed and shaking as if he had a fever. He opened his eyes and stared glassily back at her.

"Will I die?" he asked clearly.

"Bill, your leg is hurt, but there's nothing else the matter with you as far as I can tell," said Nancy. "You're going to be fine." And as soon as you're all better, you're going to jail, she thought to herself.

Bill shook his head fitfully. "So you think I'm the kind of guy who advertises for dates in the Personals?" he asked.

Nancy sat up, suddenly alert. Was he finally going to tell her what was going on? "Well, that's what your ad sounded like," she said.

"Hah! That's all you know," Bill said with a laugh. "There's something big going on, Miss

Private Detective. Big money. Bigger than you'll ever see. That's why I got a little mixed up when your friend answered my ad. You see, I thought *she* had the money," he added, as if it were the most reasonable thing in the world.

"What money was that again?" Nancy asked casually.

"John's money—John's and mine. John Engas. He was my partner. Do you think my leg is broken?"

"I don't know, but if it is, I'm sure you'll heal fast," Nancy said, soothing him. "So you and John worked together? What—uh, what kind of work?"

"Making money." Bill winked at her. "The old-fashioned way." He giggled deliriously. "Oh, I guess I might as well tell you about it. It's all in the past now. You see, we had the perfect scheme *and* the perfect bank picked out—and then John had to get *her* involved."

"You must have been furious," Nancy said. Injured as he was, he still could be dangerous, she thought, so it was important to humor him.

"'Furious' isn't the word for it. You see, two years ago—it's hard to believe it's that long ago already—my buddy John and I dreamed up the perfect scheme for robbing First Lincoln in Chicago." Suddenly he glared at her. "But don't think I'm going to tell you what it was. Oh, no! I don't want you stealing my ideas."

Nancy shook her head. She couldn't think of any way to answer that.

"So then John said he wanted his girlfriend to be our getaway driver. He said Jenny was a great driver and not the nervous type." Bill coughed. He was shivering again.

"Not the nervous type," Nancy prompted him.

"Well, that's what he said. I only saw Jenny twice. Once when we rehearsed the drive and then again on the day of the robbery. She was gorgeous, as far as I could tell—but she was wearing sunglasses, so it was kind of hard to see what she really looked like. She was dressed all in white both times—John said that was what she always wore."

Nancy could see the headlights of an approaching car—the first she'd seen since they'd been there. She was about to jump out and try to flag it down when she stopped herself. There would have to be another car at some point, and she wanted to hear the rest of Bill's story while he was still in a talkative mood. She watched silently as the car passed them and sped on into the night. Bill didn't even notice it.

"So. The robbery went fine—better than fine, actually. We had it set up so that John and Jenny would leave in one car and I'd leave in another. That way it would be harder for people to chase us. We were going to meet outside the city and

111

split up the money. That little weasel!" he suddenly shouted. "I can't believe she tricked us like that."

"What did she do?"

"Only got John killed, that's all. I waited for three hours at the spot we'd arranged. Then I heard on the car radio that—that there'd been an accident. John's car had been totaled, and he was dead."

"And Jenny?"

"John was the only person they found in the car."

"So Jenny must have escaped?" Nancy said.

"Escaped and taken the money with her." Bill sighed heavily. "I never found out who identified the body. I couldn't do it myself, of course."

"So there you were, without the money and without any idea of where Jenny was," said Nancy, trying to sound as sympathetic as she could.

"That's right—until last year. Then a—well, let's say a friend of mine told me Jenny was hiding out here. I figured she'd be using a different name and keeping out of the way, but I knew one thing about her: she and John had met through the Personals. Now, you can change your name, but reading the Personals is the kind of thing you never change. Besides, I couldn't think of any other way to reach her."

"So *that's* why you ran the ad," said Nancy.

"Yeah. The funny thing is, that's how I got my

job, too. The first copy of the *Record* I bought had a Help Wanted ad for a guy in the *Record*'s own mailroom. It's not much of a job, but it'll keep me going until I get that money back."

"But what makes you think you're going to get the money back?" Nancy asked.

"I talked to Jenny this morning."

"What? But last night—"

"No, she didn't make it to her meeting with you last night. But she called the paper again today, and I just happened to be passing by the desk when the phone rang. Lena's out sick, they said. I figured Jenny might try again, so I kept checking the phone."

He chuckled contentedly. "She's scared out of her mind by those ads I've been running. She says she'd rather turn herself in than have me looking for her. We were going to meet tomorrow. . . ."

Bill had been talking with more and more animation in the past few minutes, but now his eyes suddenly clouded. He collapsed back down into the seat. "Only *now* how can I get anywhere to meet her?" he said disgustedly. "Even if we do get rescued soon, I'm hurt too badly to go anywhere but a hospital. And then I'm as good as in jail. I have the worst luck in the world."

"I can think of one way out," Nancy said slowly. "But you may not like it."

"Well, what is it?" Bill asked.

"You can let me meet Jenny for you."

Bill stared at her. "But she could be a murderer!" he said. "She'll kill you for sure if she finds out you know what's going on!"

"That's a risk I'll have to take," Nancy answered. "I've got to finish up this case. And if I have to face a murderer to do it, that's just the way it'll have to be."

Chapter

Fourteen

So YOU'RE REALLY meeting this woman to-night?" said Bess. Nancy had stopped by Bess's house to tell her and George what had happened the night before. "I hope you know what you're doing, Nancy."

"I do," Nancy said. "There's no way Bill's going to be able to do it, and someone has to connect with Jenny—if only to make sure she's caught. Bill says he realizes he may have to go to jail, but he won't even mind as long as Jenny gets whatever treatment he does."

George snorted. "He won't mind going to jail? After everything he's done to get that money back? Do you really believe him?"

"I wouldn't," admitted Nancy, "but I think his accident really knocked the stuffing out of him. He's an incredible hypochondriac, for one thing. He really thinks that fall down the cliff was a brush with death. And he says the fact that I was the one who rescued him just proves that he was never meant to get away with this."

That wasn't all Bill had said the night before. Once Nancy had convinced him that she'd be able to handle a meeting with Jenny, he'd really gone to pieces.

"You're being so good to me after everything I've done to you," he'd said. "I'll never be able to thank you, Nancy. I swear, I'll spend the rest of my life trying to make it up to you—"

"Hold it, Bill," Nancy had said, half amused. "I have to warn you, I'm still not exactly on your side. As soon as the police get here"—the motorist they'd flagged down had promised to drive to the police station two exits away—"you're going to be in custody, you know."

But Bill had seemed resigned to that. "It feels good to have this all off my chest." He'd sighed. "I guess I'm just glad to be out of the whole mess."

The police had taken Bill and Nancy to the hospital, and Bill had been taken away for X rays. By then he was delirious again, and the nurse Nancy spoke to was sure the hospital wouldn't need to use any extra security to keep him in his room. *"He's* not going anywhere," she'd said, "not with that leg and that fever."

Now it was almost noon the next day, and Nancy was stretched out on Bess's couch. The rain had finally stopped, and sun was dancing in through the curtains. It was hard to believe she'd ever been drenched and cold.

But Bess hadn't stopped fussing since Nancy had walked through the door. "I just don't think you should meet Jenny alone, Nan." She was fretting now. "She could be a killer, for all you know—look what happened to her boyfriend!"

"Look, Bess, it's going to go just fine," Nancy said again. "We're meeting in a public place, you know."

"Yeah—the same restaurant where Bill met *me!* And look how that turned out! I'm only telling you what you told me, by the way."

Nancy leaned over and pinched her friend's cheek affectionately. "I know," she said. "And I appreciate your concern. I think I'll be able to handle things, though. From what Bill said, Jenny's much too spooked to try anything.

"Now give me one more cup of coffee before I go," she continued, holding out her cup to George. "And some more of that coffeecake, if Bess hasn't finished it. Otherwise I'll fall asleep right here and never get to the paper at all."

She wasn't meeting Jenny till that night, so Nancy had decided to stop in at the *Record* and fill Mr. Whittaker in on what had happened. After that she'd head back to the hospital to visit Ned. It had been torture the night before, being in the same building with Ned and knowing she couldn't see him—visiting hours had been long over by the time she and Bill had gotten there. Now, though, Nancy hoped to make up for it.

"In the hospital!" Mr. Whittaker exclaimed half an hour later. "What's the matter with him?"

"You're not going to like this, Mr. Whittaker. Bill's the one who's been running those ads. He's also the one who phoned in that bomb threat yesterday." Quickly Nancy filled him in on what had happened since she had last seen him. When she had finished, Mr. Whittaker's face was purple with rage.

"I'd like to go over there and break his other leg for him!" he growled. "When I think of what could have happened yesterday if anyone had panicked—not to mention what he's done to you and to this paper's reputation—well, I'm glad you're handling this case and not me."

"I hope it will all be over soon, Mr. Whittaker. And, please, don't mention anything about this until Jenny's in custody. We don't want her to get word of what's going on. Now, if it's okay with you, I'd like to go talk to Lena. I owe her an apology for a few things. And then I have to go to the hospital to see Ned."

"Sure. Do anything you want," answered Mr. Whittaker. "I'm completely in your debt."

"No, I mean it. You look a lot better," Nancy told Ned.

It was true. Ned looked thinner, and his face was tired and gaunt. But the feverish brightness was gone from his eyes, and he was talking like himself again.

"I see your fans haven't forgotten you. This is *lovely,*" Nancy went on, picking up the ugliest flower arrangement she'd ever seen. It was a china vase shaped like a donkey and filled with huge mustard-colored chrysanthemums. A balloon that said "For a Good Boy" was tied to the donkey's neck.

Ned grinned. "Oh, that's from George and Bess. They thought it would cheer me up. I kind of hope one of them ends up in the hospital someday so I can send it to *her.*

"They think I'll be able to leave in a few more days," he added.

"So you're really getting better?" Nancy asked.

"Oh, I'm a star patient. I may have to do a little physical therapy to get my legs back in shape."

"Well, I'll help you," Nancy said quickly. "I'll work you harder than your coaches ever did."

"*Sure* you will," Ned answered. He took her hand in his. "I've really missed you, Nancy. Not seeing you on top of having to eat hospital food is

119

just too much. Do you think you can come to see me again tonight? Evening visiting hours start at seven."

Nancy's heart sank. "Oh, Ned, I'd—I'd love to, but I've got something else on."

"A date?" Ned asked teasingly.

"Well, just with a—a girl I know." It was so hard not to tell him about the case!

Ned gave a theatrical sigh. "That's just the way of the world, I guess," he said, his voice vibrating with mock sorrow. "A guy's in the hospital for a few hours and his girlfriend forgets all about him."

"Stop!" Nancy said, more sharply than she had meant to. "You know I'd come to see you if I could. This is something I can't get out of."

"Hey, I was only kidding!" Ned protested.

Nancy bent down and kissed him. "I know," she said, tracing his mouth with her finger. "I just feel bad about it. I wish I didn't have to leave at all."

"Well, you're welcome to stay as long as you like," Ned said.

Nancy laughed. "I don't think the doctor would like *that.*" She bent to kiss him again. "I'll see you tomorrow, the minute they let me in," she said.

Back out in the hall, Nancy paused for a minute. Visiting hours were almost over, but she had promised herself she'd stop in to see Bill. She didn't know what floor he was on, though.

She'd have to go down to the Emergency Room to see where they'd sent him.

"Bill Stark—Bill Stark," the nurse at the reception desk repeated, checking a list of new patients. "I'm sorry, but I don't see his name here."

"He came into the ER last night," Nancy said. "Could you just check one more time?"

"Wait a minute. The man the police brought in—the one who'd hurt his leg?" the nurse asked, looking more closely at Nancy. "Are you that private investigator who came in with him?"

"Yes. I'm Nancy Drew. Is there some kind of problem?"

The nurse winced. "You could say that. He —well, he seems to have left the hospital. When the resident checked his bed this morning, he was gone."

Chapter

Fifteen

*G*ONE?" NANCY REPEATED blankly. "But he
wasn't supposed to go anywhere! He's commit-
ted a crime!"

"Ms. Drew, we're aware of that. I can't tell you
how sorry we all are. No one here thought there
was the slightest chance he'd be able even to get
out of his bed—he was in such terrible shape
when he came in. We've informed the police, of
course, and they're looking for him."

"But I just don't understand how he could
have done it," Nancy said. "Wasn't his leg broken?"

The nurse sighed. "Actually, no. The X rays didn't show a fracture. He may have bruised the bone—that can be very painful—but nothing more serious than that. He hadn't even sprained his ankle."

"Well, that's one piece of good news," Nancy said bitterly.

"If you'd like to talk to the doctor who treated him last night—"

"I can't," Nancy interrupted. "All of this means I've got to change my plans a little. Thanks for telling me," she said.

So Bill was in hiding somewhere, she thought as she raced out to her car. Everything he'd told her about accepting his fate had been a lie.

And that might mean that he was going to try to reach Jenny before Nancy did. If he did want revenge after all—

"I can't let him get to her," she said aloud. It was true that Jenny had broken the law, but Nancy knew it was still her job to protect Jenny. If she was guilty of anything, the law—not Bill Stark—should punish her. Besides, the money Bill had stolen had to be returned to the Chicago bank he'd taken it from. If Jenny gave it to him, that would never happen.

Without realizing it, Nancy had started driving on the road that would take her to Bel Canto, the restaurant where she was supposed to meet Jenny. She checked her watch. It would be after six o'clock by the time she got there. Jenny wasn't due until seven, but Nancy would be able to use the extra time to make sure Bill wasn't lurking around.

The restaurant parking lot had hardly any cars in it. I don't know how they stay in business, Nancy thought as she parked the Mustang.

Bill's car certainly wouldn't be here. It had probably been taken to a junkyard already. The other cars in the parking lot looked empty. Nancy walked through the lot, peering into each one. Unless Bill was hiding in one of the trunks, he wasn't inside any of these cars.

Nancy walked around to the back of the restaurant, but the only vehicle there was a Bel Canto van. Nancy quickly swung open its back door and looked inside, hoping no one from the restaurant would choose that moment to come outside. No Bill—just three crates of carrots.

Okay, he wasn't out here. Nancy walked into the restaurant and checked out the tables. Two elderly women having an early dinner; a mother and her teenage daughter; a few businessmen having drinks; and that was it.

"I'm supposed to be meeting a friend here," Nancy told the waiter as he walked up to her. "Two friends, actually. A blond girl and a tall blond guy who walks with a limp. I guess they're not here yet?"

"No, no one's come in for the last half hour or

so," the waiter answered. "Would you like something from the bar while you're waiting?"

"A ginger ale, please." Nancy took a seat at a window table facing the door.

Ten minutes later she had memorized the fly-specked menu and was beginning to wish she'd brought a magazine along. It was still early, but what if Jenny didn't show up at all? What if Bill had already tracked her down? How would Nancy be able to track *him* down? I certainly didn't need to get here early, Nancy thought irritably. I may be sitting here for—

At that moment a frail-looking blonde with enormous blue eyes opened the front door and peered timidly inside. She was wearing white pants and a white blazer and carrying an oversize shoulder bag. It looked as if it was heavy. Nancy sprang to her feet and walked up to her.

"Jenny?" she said.

The girl nodded. "Yes," she said, her voice scarcely louder than a whisper, "but where's —where's Bill? Who are you?"

"My name is Nancy Drew. I don't know if Bill's going to be able to meet you." Quickly Nancy explained what had happened to him and why she was there.

For a minute Jenny didn't seem to understand. "Well, where is he now?" she asked.

"That's just the problem," Nancy said. "I don't really know. I think you and I should probably get out of here pretty fast, in case he's on his way."

"Oh, no, what am I going to do? Now that you've told me all this, I know he'll kill me!" Jenny moaned. She was swaying on her feet. Nancy grabbed her elbow to steady her.

"He won't have a chance to get near you," Nancy reassured her. "Come and sit down for a minute. Waiter"—she beckoned to him—"could you bring us some tea? I'll pay you for it now. I'm afraid we won't be staying for dinner."

At the table Jenny buried her face in her hands. "It's all so terrible," she said as if to herself. "I can't believe I'm even involved in something like this."

"Can you tell me a little about it?" Nancy asked sympathetically. "I've only heard Bill's side of the story."

Jenny sighed. "I'm sure whatever he's told you about me is true. That's what's been so horrible —knowing that he was right to be so mad at me."

"He hasn't said much about you," Nancy said carefully. She didn't want to scare Jenny even more. "Just that you were John's girlfriend, and you were driving John away when there was some kind of accident. And that he—he lost track of you after that."

"I don't know why I ever said I'd do it," Jenny said. "I'd always known John was doing something illegal, but I never asked him what. I guess I didn't really want to find out. That would have meant I'd have to break up with him, and I couldn't stand the thought of that."

Nancy nodded.

"When he told me about the bank job, he promised it was a one-time thing. It would give us enough money to settle down, and he'd never do it again." Jenny's eyes filled with tears. "Well, he was right about never doing it again."

She lifted her head and stared at the wall as if replaying the long-ago scene in her mind. "John was so careful about everything! I didn't think we really needed to rehearse the drive, but he insisted. He didn't want me to get flustered, he said.

"It all went like a dream," she continued. "He and Bill drove themselves over there in Bill's car, and I pulled up in front of the bank at exactly ten-fifteen. There they were, just coming out the door. John jumped into the car, I took off, we drove for a couple of blocks, and then—and then—" She was knotting her hands together so hard her knuckles were white.

"And then?" asked Nancy gently.

"Then—if you can believe it—I ran a red light. Such a stupid thing to do after all that practice!" Jenny shivered. "I'll never forget the sight of that truck coming toward us, or the sound it made when it hit our car. It came right through the passenger door. Then there was this

127

incredible bang when the car in back of us rear-ended us. I—I looked over at John, and —well, you wouldn't have needed a doctor to tell that he was dead. The briefcase with the money was still in his hand."

Jenny broke off again. Her face was flushed now. "This is the part I still can't believe I did. It was like a silent movie or something. I just reached down and took the briefcase out of his hand. Then I got out of the car and walked away."

"And nobody saw you?" Nancy asked incredulously.

"I don't think anyone was looking at me," Jenny said simply. "You can't imagine what that intersection had turned into. It wasn't only our car that had been rear-ended—a car had driven into the back of the truck, too. No one was paying attention to *me.*"

It was getting dark, and the restaurant was starting to fill up now. The waiter darted an anxious look at their table, probably wondering when they'd leave. But Jenny was oblivious to everything except her story.

"Well, so now I had all that money," she went on, "and no John. I just went home and put the briefcase under my bed. Then I went to work. I'd called in earlier and said I'd be late."

"And what did you do with the money?"

"Nothing, for a year. I just left it under my

bed. I didn't even want to touch it. Then it got so I couldn't stand to be in that apartment anymore. I had to start all over. I used a little of the money to move to River Heights. The rest of it's still under my bed.

"To tell you the truth, I was almost relieved when I realized Bill was after me," Jenny said. "It was worse wondering when he'd find me. Never knowing what was going to happen. At least I can settle things with him now. That's why I decided to call the paper. I was so flustered that I didn't realize there was no coffee shop at Fortieth and East anymore. I thought, at least I'd be able to stop running. It's not as bad as—"

There was a gentle tapping at the window. Both girls looked up, startled.

Bill Stark waved cheerily at them, his face ghostlike against the dark night.

"Oh, my God!" Jenny gasped. "He'll kill us!" She was already on her feet and moving toward the back door. Nancy was right next to her.

"My car's out back," Jenny panted. "If we go out the back door, we may be able to—"

Just then she stumbled against one of the tables. She dropped her shoulder bag, and its contents spilled all over the floor. Jenny fell to her knees and began frantically scooping everything up.

"Just leave it all there and take your bag," Nancy said sharply, jerking Jenny to her feet. "Here's the back door."

The parking lot was dark and deserted, and Bill Stark was walking toward them.

"Hi, gals," he said.

This time he *did* have a gun. He pulled it out of his pocket and aimed it right at Nancy's face.

Chapter

Sixteen

Okay, Jenny," Bill said. "Tie her up."

Before Nancy could move, Jenny had grabbed her, stuffed Nancy's mouth with a rag that Bill had thrown her, and tied another rag over it. At the same time Bill was opening the trunk of a battered red Honda.

What was going on? Jenny seemed to have become another person! She was pinning Nancy's arms behind her back so tightly that she couldn't even think about wriggling away. Not that she was going to try—not with that .38 pointed at her. The gun didn't waver as Jenny dragged Nancy over to the trunk and pushed her inside.

As Bill was closing the trunk, he leaned over Nancy. "I thought you'd like to know that there's been a little change in plans," he said politely. "Jenny and I have decided to work together for the time being. You see, she actually *did* show up at Fortieth and East right about the time I'd, uh, put you out of commission, and we thought we might as well pool our resources."

So this whole meeting with Jenny had been a setup. Nancy felt sick.

"Sorry I put you to so much trouble yesterday," Bill continued. "I guess I just overreacted to the pain. You know me—Mr. Walking Wounded. Don't make any noise in there, or I'll come around and shoot you." He smiled and slammed the door, and Nancy heard him turn the key in the lock.

The Honda started up with a roar. Whoever was driving was flooring it. Nancy rolled helplessly back and forth as the car whipped around turns and sped out of the parking lot.

Nancy forced herself not to panic. She'd been in this situation before, and there was definitely no sense in struggling. If the trunk was airtight, she'd only use up oxygen. And she didn't know this part of River Heights well, so trying to figure out where the car was going wouldn't help her. The only thing she could do was try to relax.

She was furious at herself. Furious for trusting Bill and furious for having believed Jenny's story. They'd fed her a piece of the truth, and she'd believed it was the whole thing. How could she have been so gullible?

But wouldn't anyone have trusted them? she asked herself. Bill hadn't been faking the agony he'd been in the day before—even though he had managed to conceal part of the truth from her. And Nancy was sure Jenny's story was pretty close to the truth—at least her description of the events leading up to John's death. But keeping the money unspent under her bed seemed a little unlikely to Nancy now.

She winced as the car bounced over what felt like an enormous pothole. Had she been in there for a few seconds or for hours? It was hard to tell. Her whole body ached from being jolted back and forth, and it was frighteningly hot and stuffy in the trunk. Worst of all was the cottony feel of the gag in her mouth.

Nancy wondered if she dared take it off. After all, they hadn't tied her hands. But Bill had a gun, and she'd better not make him mad.

At least she could retie the gag so it was more comfortable. Nancy yanked it off—luckily Bill hadn't knotted it very well—and tied it so that it wasn't cutting into her face. She'd just finished knotting it when the car stopped.

Nancy heard the car door slamming. Footsteps coming toward her. The trunk being unlocked.

And then Bill was standing there, pointing the gun in her face. Nancy stared at him, making no attempt to move.

"Good girl," said Bill approvingly. "Glad to see you behaved yourself in there. Now, I'm going to take this gag off you, but I don't want you making a sound. Not one sound. Understand?"

Nancy nodded, and Bill pulled off the gag. Then he grabbed Nancy's hand and dragged her out of the car.

They were in a dark little alley next to the *Record* building. "Jenny, you want to come in or wait?" Bill asked.

"Might as well come in," said Jenny casually as she got out of the car. "I've never seen a newspaper office before."

"Okay. Let's go." Bill nudged Nancy's shoulder with the gun. "We're going in a side door," he told her. "I want you to act completely normal. If anyone sees us and asks what we're doing here, tell them this is part of your investigation. Otherwise, I don't want a word out of you."

The entrance he took her through was a set of heavy black double doors at the back of the building. The three of them stepped into a dimly lit hall. Ahead of them was a service elevator.

"It wasn't a great job, working here, but I guess it came in handy," Bill said with a chuckle. "All the mailroom deliveries come in this way. I've got keys to everything," he added, answering Nancy's unspoken question.

He unlocked the service elevator, and it slid open with a rusty wheeze. "After you, ladies,"

Bill said as he shoved Nancy in. The barred elevator door clicked shut, and the elevator creaked slowly to the fifth floor—the newsroom.

"All ready and waiting, I see," said Bill approvingly. In the dark the room was filled with the day's leftovers—the computers waiting silently for someone to use them, a "Do This First!" memo slapped on top of a pile of papers on someone's desk, a bicycle wheel whose owner must have decided to walk home. Far below them Nancy could hear the roar of the presses. They'd be making too much noise for anyone working down there to hear her.

With a flourish Bill pulled out the chair at the nearest terminal. "Have a seat," he said chattily to Nancy. "You, too, Jenny. Let's talk."

Her face expressionless, Jenny plunked herself down at the next terminal and fixed her gaze on Nancy.

"Well, I got to thinking after you left the hospital last night," Bill said. "You know, I'm a pretty nice guy, but I do have one fault—I talk too much when I'm upset.

"So I said to myself," he continued, " 'Why let a little pain stop me from getting what I want?' Especially when my leg wasn't broken after all. With all this money at stake, it'd be crazy to let a bad attitude get in my way." He sounded as if he were giving some kind of screwball pep talk.

"So I called Jenny last night and told her about you. We decided that since you knew about both of us, she and I would be in this together now. So that's why we're leaving town together."

"With the bank money," said Nancy. "How much is left, Jenny?"

Jenny grinned wryly. "Enough," she said. "It should cover expenses for a while, anyway." A shadow crossed her face. "Of course it won't go as far divided in half, but what can I say? Bill's a very persuasive guy."

"I guess I am," said Bill. His smile was sinister. Nancy wondered just what he'd said to convince Jenny she should join forces with him. "Well, we've got one problem before we can take off—and Nancy, you can probably figure out what that is."

"Me, I'll bet," answered Nancy.

"Uh-huh. You're the only person who knows about us. I guess that means you'll just have to get out of here somehow."

"'Get out of here'? What a delicate way of putting it, Bill," Nancy answered coolly. Her heart was hammering in her chest, but she wasn't going to show it. Jenny had found a compact in somebody's desk and was looking at herself approvingly before turning her attention back to Nancy.

"Besides, I'm *not* the only person who knows what you're up to," Nancy continued. "My two best friends do, too. Of course Bess already feels pretty close to you, but George can't *wait* to meet you. I told them to call the police if they hadn't heard from me by nine this evening." She'd just noticed that the clock in back of Bill said 8:48. "I also filled Mr. Whittaker in this afternoon. In fact"—she was desperately trying to think of something that would sound plausible—"he's probably got this room under some kind of surveillance right now."

"Good try, Nancy. Not quite believable, but if it's true, that's all the more reason for finishing things up quickly. Your friends can be the first to read your ad in tomorrow's Personals column."

"My ad?"

"Yeah." Bill reached over and switched on her computer. "Don't worry. I'll dictate it. All you'll have to do is type it.

"Don't make any mistakes, now," he commanded. "We don't want any typos in your last words."

Chapter

Seventeen

TIME FROZE IN the empty room. Nancy felt as if she couldn't breathe. The humming of the computer seemed unbearably loud, and somewhere outside a train whistled in the night.

Bill looked up at the ceiling as if searching for inspiration. "Let's see," he said, "how should we start this? 'I, Nancy Drew, have decided to end it all'? It's not quite in the general style of the Personals, but—"

"Wait. There's still one thing I never found out," said Nancy rapidly. If she could keep talking, maybe she'd survive a little longer. "Why *was* John's body found in the driver's seat, Jenny? I thought you'd been driving the car."

Jenny's laugh was horrifyingly happy. "Of course I was driving the car! But it wasn't hard switching places with him. I mean, he was a little heavy. A dead weight, you might say"—she laughed merrily again—"but, Nancy, I really think people can accomplish anything they set their minds to, don't you?"

Nancy couldn't hold back a shudder. Jenny's composure was inhuman—and she was obviously even more cold-blooded than Bill.

"I mean," Jenny prattled on, "why *shouldn't* people think John had been driving? He wasn't going to be able to tell them any diff—"

"That's enough of that," Bill cut in harshly. He waved the gun at Nancy. "Come on, start typing."

There was nothing else she could do.

"You can put it in your own words," Bill added. Tell them—tell them—say you've realized how much trouble your job has caused other people. Got that?"

"Got it," Nancy said, typing away.

"Now say that you can't live with the guilt any longer, and you've decided to end it all."

"End—it—all," Nancy repeated. "Okay. Now what?"

"Just type 'Goodbye.'"

"Done," Nancy said after a second.

"Give it to me." He read it quickly. "Good. I'll get it into the paper later. And now—Jenny, hold her down."

Jenny's hands clamped down on Nancy's shoulders before Nancy could even think of moving.

Bill lifted the gun and put it to her temple.

In that split second, a picture flashed into Nancy's mind. She saw herself jabbing an elbow into Jenny's midsection, bringing down Bill's arm with a karate chop, grabbing the gun, and saving herself. It all looked beautifully simple the way she pictured it.

But it was just a flash of what might have been. She was still sitting in the chair, and the gun was cold against her skin.

"Say your prayers," Bill told her. "You've got ten seconds. One—two—"

"Wait a minute," Jenny interrupted him. "If she's supposed to be ending it all, why don't we push her out of the window? That would look a lot more like suicide."

"But it's only four stories down," protested Bill.

Jenny shrugged. "So what? If she falls head-first—"

Bill paused for a heart-shattering second to think about it. Then he put the gun down.

"You know, you're right," he said. "The window it is. Nancy, there's been another change in plans."

Nancy leaped to her feet—but Bill was quicker. He grabbed her arms and pinned them behind her. "Break the window," he said over his shoulder to Jenny.

Instantly Jenny picked up a chair and smashed it against the huge pane of glass. For a second the sheet of glass hung there, miraculously intact. Then it collapsed, shivering into thousands of fragments. A gust of cold air billowed into the room.

"Let's go," Bill said to Nancy. And slowly he began marching her toward that jagged black hole.

Nancy saw he'd forgotten the gun! It was still on the desk. With a strength she'd never known she had, she wrenched herself out of his hands and flung herself at the gun. It skidded across the desk and fell harmlessly to the floor. Nancy lunged toward it—and picked it up.

"All right. Back off. Both of you," she snapped.

Slowly Bill and Jenny raised their hands into the air, then backed away.

"Sit," Nancy ordered.

Slowly they sank into chairs. Nancy took a step forward. "Now, I'm going to call the police," she said. "And building security. Don't either one of you dare move."

Suddenly Jenny let out an ear-shattering shriek.

Startled, Nancy lowered her arm for a second. That was all the time Bill needed. He vaulted from his seat, kicked the gun out of her hand, and picked it up himself.

"Good job, Jenny," he said. "Now let's start all over again."

He was pushing her inexorably closer to the window. One step, now two. The cold air from outside beckoned her toward its chilly embrace.

Three steps. One piece of glass that hadn't fallen suddenly slipped to the ground.

I never got to say goodbye to Ned, Nancy thought. Or my father.

Jenny grabbed her hand and pulled her forward. "You pull, I'll push," said Bill.

Now Nancy could see the street below. It wasn't so far to fall. She was struggling as hard as she could, but it was like being underwater.

"Help me, somebody!" she screamed out the window.

"Out we go," said Bill, and pushed.

Nancy toppled forward into the dark air and plummeted toward the ground.

Chapter

Eighteen

THE MINUTE NANCY was out the window she kicked her legs down like a diver so that she wouldn't land on her head. That—and a window ledge on the fourth floor—were all that saved her. She fell onto the ledge, started to roll off, and hurled herself back against the wall.

Gasping, she looked up at the fifth floor—and saw Bill and Jenny peering down at her. "That was a stupid move," Jenny said calmly. "Why don't you just face facts?"

Her face disappeared from the window for a second—and when she came back she was holding the .38.

"Let go and jump," she ordered, "or I'll shoot."

Nancy glanced down. Below her, cars moved steadily back and forth. They don't know I'm here, she thought. No one can help me.

"I'm waiting," Jenny said.

Nancy stared back up at her. "I don't want to sound like someone in the movies," she called, "but you really won't get away with this."

"Want to bet?" Jenny leveled the gun so it was pointing straight at Nancy's head.

If I stay here, she'll shoot me for sure, Nancy thought rapidly. I've got a better chance of making it if I jump.

She closed her eyes and jumped.

"Nancy!" screeched a familiar voice behind her. "Oh, my God—she's dead!"

I am? Nancy slowly opened her eyes. She had landed in the thin fringe of shrubbery bordering the *Record* building. Her arms and legs were scratched, but the bushes had broken her fall. And Bess and George were running toward her.

Bess's car was parked right in front of the building. A police car was pulling up behind it, its siren screaming.

"Are you okay, Ms. Drew?" one of the officers shouted as he leaped from his car.

"I—I guess I *am* all right," Nancy said with a shaky laugh. "Get me out of this bush, will you?"

"Oh, Nancy!" Bess was crying openly as she and George dragged Nancy out. "I can't believe we got here in time! When we saw you fall, we thought—you want a tissue?"

"No, you do," Nancy answered, giving them both a big hug. "*I* want to know how you got here in time. But first I want those guys up there arrested."

"I kind of think that's what's happening now," George said, gesturing at the *Record*'s front door. The two policemen were just vanishing inside. "There are more police out back. There's no place those creeps can go."

"Let's just sit in the car and wait for them, then," said Nancy. "I'm not leaving until I'm sure they haven't wiggled away again."

"Well, we butted in," said George cheerfully once they'd climbed into the car, "but I can't say I'm sorry. Bess was fussing about you all day—"

"Not *fussing,* George!" Bess put in indignantly. "I was *right* to be worried."

"Yes, I guess for once you were," George answered. "Anyway, Nan, after a lot of discussion, we decided to follow you to the restaurant. When Bess saw Bill there, I knew she *had* been right to worry. We followed his car here and called the police when we saw him take you inside. That's all. Are you mad at us?"

"Are you kidding?" Nancy snorted. "I just wish you'd managed to make those bushes a little thicker. I'm all banged up, you know— Look! There they are!"

Bill and Jenny—in handcuffs—were being hustled down the steps. "What's he saying?" Nancy asked. "Roll down the window, Bess."

"Police brutality! I'll sue the whole department!" Bill was roaring. "I'm in agony! I think my ribs are broken!"

Then he caught sight of Nancy. "This is all *her* fault! If she hadn't come snooping around here, none of this would have happened! It's entrapment!"

Jenny had been silent during all of this. But as she passed Bess's car, she gave Nancy a wry little salute. There was a look almost like respect in her eyes.

"Take a look, Bess," Nancy murmured. "That's the girl Bill's been looking for all this time."

Bess shuddered. "Looks like a match made in heaven," she said.

"I can't go to jail!" Bill was shouting. "I'm a sick man! You've got to take me to the hospital!"

"Yeah, yeah," said the trooper. "We heard that you had a pretty good time in the hospital. I think you'll live without another visit."

"Bess, roll up the window again," begged Nancy. "If I hear another word out of him, I think I'll explode."

"Glad to," said Bess.

Then Nancy remembered. The hospital! "Ned!" Nancy gasped. "We've got to get right over there and see him—"

"Ms. Drew?" The officer who had spoken to her earlier was leaning his head into the car window. "We were wondering if we could get a statement from you now."

"A statement. Of course." Nancy sighed. "I guess Ned will have to wait. Bess, can you take me down to the station?"

Bess patted her shoulder comfortingly. "No problem. Anyway, Nan, visiting hours have been over for—well, for hours. You can get some beauty sleep and go over there first thing in the morning."

"And *now*," George added, "you can fill us in on exactly what happened to you tonight."

"So *that's* what you were doing last night," said Ned the next day. Nancy was perched on the side of his bed. "Some date!" he went on. "I guess I can stop worrying about the competition."

"Oh, I don't know," Nancy answered. "A blond, blue-eyed psychopath who's also an incredible complainer and a complete coward? Maybe he's just the guy for me."

"You should have answered that ad instead of Bess, then," said Ned.

Before coming into Ned's room, Nancy had

147

hunted down the doctor who'd asked her not to talk about the case with Ned. "Do you think it would be okay to do it now?" she asked wistfully.

"Oh, I can't see that it would do any harm," answered the doctor. "He's making a very quick recovery—and anyway, the case is all over now, isn't it?"

It was, though Nancy still couldn't quite believe it. Things had all happened so quickly! Bill and Jenny were being charged with robbery, aggravated assault—and, in Jenny's case, manslaughter. It seemed she might have staged that "accident" after the robbery just to get her boyfriend out of the way.

Now she and Bill were out of the way themselves. Nancy was glad of that, of course. But she couldn't shut out one tiny, nagging worry. Had it all been worth it?

"What's the matter?" Ned asked. "You're a million miles away—and it doesn't look like much fun."

"I guess I'm wondering what I accomplished this time," Nancy said. "Sure, I helped catch two people who should be behind bars. But that was really just luck. If Bess hadn't answered that ad—if Bill hadn't had that car accident—if Bess and George hadn't come at just the right time —everything could have been completely different. It seems to me that *I* didn't do anything except get your head hurt for you."

"Nancy, Nancy," Ned said, stroking her cheek. "That's not true. You make your own luck. If you hadn't been a girl who looks out for her friends, you'd never have investigated the paper at all. If you hadn't already solved a case involving one of his reporters, Mr. Whittaker would never have let you prowl around the paper. And if you hadn't helped Bill get out of the woods even after he attacked you, he never would have confessed to robbing the bank. None of it would have happened if you weren't the kind of person you are.

"As for getting me hurt," Ned continued, "I don't want to hear you talking like that."

"But it wouldn't have happened if I weren't a detective—"

"But if you weren't a detective, you wouldn't be Nancy Drew. And Nancy Drew's the girl I happen to be in love with." He reached up and kissed her.

"Well," Nancy said after a second, "if you'll just tell me you'll be able to go back to the playing field, I'll be completely happy."

"But I will! Didn't the doctor tell you? There's no lasting injury at all. I should be completely back to normal."

Nancy leaned against him with a long, happy sigh. "Okay," she said. "Now we can stop talking business."

* * *

"Took you long enough," Bess complained as Nancy floated into the waiting room. "What's the matter—did he hurt his head again?"

Nancy just beamed at her. "He's fine. More than fine."

"When will he be out of the hospital?" George inquired.

"Tomorrow morning! We'll still have plenty of time before he has to go back to school—he's taking an additional week off to recover."

"In that case," said Bess, "we'd better try to do a lot today. Once he's out of the hospital, we'll never see you again. And let's start by going out for brunch somewhere. I'm absolutely starving."

George chuckled. "Let's see. If Bess wrote her own ad for the Personals, how would it go? 'Hungry girl looking for a guy with deep pockets. Let's meet over lunch and—'"

"You're cruel!" Bess said, and threw her nose into the air. "After all, I have to eat today because tomorrow I'm going on a diet!"

And the three friends burst into laughter.

Nancy's next case:

When Ned burns the barbecue, Nancy offers him a real culinary challenge—a course at the famed Claude DuPres International Cooking School. Bess will delve into the delights of French pastry with stunning young chef Jacques Bonet, and George is to try her hand at Chinese food. But the session is barely underway when Chef DuPres collapses. Could he have been poisoned?

Then Ned finds Chef Trent Richards frozen solid in the meat locker. Everyone's top suspect is Chef Paul Slesak, until he announces that someone has been rifling through his secret recipes. When Nancy and her friends get a look at them, they realize that the ingredients contain a code linked to the passing of international secrets—and the next exchange will take place at a dinner that DuPres and Bonet are catering.

Which chef is the real traitor? And can Nancy and Ned stop him before he completes his mission? Find out in *RECIPE FOR MURDER*, Case #21 in The Nancy Drew Files®.